Doris Fein:
Quartz Boyar

Doris Fein:
Quartz Boyar

T. Ernesto Bethancourt

Holiday House/New York

Library of Congress Cataloging in Publication Data

Bethancourt, T Ernesto.
    Doris Fein, quartz boyar.

    Sequel to Doris Fein, superspy.
    SUMMARY: When she arrives in Paris transporting
a coveted objet d'art for a secret government agency,
Doris Fein finds herself caught up in a net of inter-
national intrigue.
    [1. Spy stories]   I. Title.
PZ7.B46627Dos   [Fic]   80–15920
ISBN 0–8234–0378–5

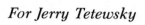

For Jerry Tetewsky

Contents

In 1952, when Dmitri Tiomkin, the distinguished motion picture composer, received the Academy Award for his masterful score to the film *High Noon,* he made a most unusual acceptance speech. He thanked not only *High Noon*'s producer, director, and stars, but went on to thank Peter Ilyich Tchaikovsky, Ludwig van Beethoven, and a half score of other classical composers. Tiomkin felt that all these writers had influenced him, and therefore were also partly responsible for his score. It was a commendable show of honesty and humility.

I should therefore like to acknowledge the influence of the following sources in the writing of this book: the Saturday matinees at the Oasis Theatre in Brooklyn—two features, five cartoons, and the latest installment of a cliff-hanging serial. I would also like to thank the many wonderful, talented people who wrote, directed, and acted in those murky black-and-white Warner Brothers' films of the 1940s. It is to them and to those films that this book is intended as a loving valentine.

T. E. BETHANCOURT

Huntington Beach
California, 1980

Ekaterinburg: 1918

Ekaterinburg: 1918

Alex knew that something was wrong. Dreadfully, hurtingly wrong. For months, ever since he and his family had moved to this house, his mother and older sisters had spoken in whispers in Alex's presence. What were they concealing? Bewildered, thirteen-year-old Alex had sought comfort in his toys and games. There were few left, for when the strange men with rough accents and rifles had come and spoken harshly to Alex's parents, the boy had been allowed to bring but a fraction of his many playthings on the long train ride.

There had been another train ride to this new house, with Alex's mother and father trying, as always, to protect the boy from any injury, no matter how slight. Alex's parents had good reasons for their actions. The slightest bruise could cause Alex to bleed uncontrollably underneath his skin. This resulted in large, purple bulges that radiated a dull, throbbing pain. They could remain for weeks, sometimes for months.

But bruises were nothing compared to a blow to a knee or elbow. Then blood would seep into the affected joint cavity, causing a swelling accompanied by such pain that often Alex would faint from its fearful intensity. Never for Alex were there games of a normal, rough-and-tumble boyhood. Such activities could prove lethal, for Alex suffered from hemophilia, the dread disease that prevents the blood from clotting.

Alex knew from birth that he was different from other children, from his own four sisters. For Alex, life had been a long succession of doctors, therapists, bodyguards, and most recently, Gregory, the wild-eyed faith healer in whom his mother had such confidence. The holy man had frightened Alex. His piercing eyes, dark as the pits of Hell, had haunted the boy's dreams. And those times when Gregory had laid hands on Alex, had touched those sore and tender parts of his underdeveloped body, ravaged by the disease, those had been the worst times of all. Alex shuddered, remembering the feel of those rough hands and, most of all, the gaze of the holy man, so magnetic that it had sapped Alex of any will to resist.

For the first time in his life, Alex had begun to lie to his parents. When his mother had asked the boy if he felt better after the visits from Gregory, Alex had claimed improvement, hoping somehow that then the treatments would end. Gregory, with his ill-kempt beard and foul personal effluvium, had been a constant source of repulsion and loathing to Alex. When, finally, Alex had been told by his mother that Gregory had "gone away and would never return," the boy had been secretly overjoyed.

It wasn't long after Gregory disappeared from Alex's life that the rough men who were rude to Alex's parents had come upon the scene. Since that time, Alex and his family had been shuttled from one place to another, always at the point of rifles. The men had spoken with accents, sometimes in languages that Alex had not been able to understand. And though his parents had tried to make a game of the events, Alex had known that their laughter was forced. It wasn't really a game at all.

Finally, the family had been forced onto still another train and brought to this house in the mountains. Now hardly able to walk, the result of a fall, Alex had been spending his days in the room where he slept, playing with the remains of his games and toys.

Once there had been countless toys of all descriptions: entire factories in miniature, powered by toy steam boilers, elaborate train sets so large that they carried full-sized dolls for passengers, jeweled and enameled puzzles, dolls, figurines, and chessmen. Of all the mighty armies of toy soldiers Alex had once possessed, only twenty-four remained. Alex, of late, had taken to carrying one of these figures with him at all times. It was as though the sick boy feared he would soon lose the last of his playthings.

On this night, Alex knew something wrong was happening. His father came to the boy's room and helped Alex put on the metal brace he now required for standing upright or hobbling across a room. As his father helped Alex to dress, he told the boy that the family was to move again. Alex tightened his clutch on the figurine he held. Sleepily, he offered no resistance when his father gathered him up in his arms and carried him downstairs to where more of the rough men were waiting.

Alex's father was forced into a small semi-basement room. As his father carried him into the small room, Alex noted that the one window in the bare cubicle was high above their heads and heavily barred. After that he began to doze. When his father called for chairs so that Alex's mother could rest, Alex was already asleep. He did not waken when his father, still cradling him in his arms, gently eased him onto a chair.

Nor did Alex stir when the rough men read to his parents from a piece of paper. He slept on as they raised loaded pistols and aimed them at his parents and family, even the two servants. He did not feel his father half rise from his chair and felt only a momentary stab of blinding pain as the bullets ripped through his father's body and penetrated his own frail frame.

Alex did not hear his mother's cry of "Oh, God, no!" nor see her make the sign of the cross in the air seconds before she, too, was riddled by the deadly fusillade. He felt no pain when one of the rough men emptied a pistol into his still breathing body.

The impact of the last bullets loosened Alex's grip on the toy soldier he had clutched so tightly earlier.

The boy's fingers opened and a small figurine, five inches in height, rolled to the floor of the basement room.

It was a figure of a boyar, a rank of nobility long abolished by Alex's remote ancestor, Peter. The haughty aristocratic bearing of the little boyar only hinted at the mighty warriors from whom Alex was descended. With its fierce bushy beard, long-sleeved caftan, high felt hat, and war-like demeanor, the diminutive boyar seemed to represent all that had been the pride of Alex's family. Where the beard, robes, and hat covered the figure, it was enameled with bright splashes of crimson and white. This did not fully conceal the fact that the tiny boyar was carved from one massive crystal of rose quartz. Only the boyar's hands, gripping a minuscule sword encrusted with *petits brillants,* and his shiny pink face, ingeniously set with sapphire blue eyes, betrayed the material from which the figure had been sculpted.

The figurine rested on a base of the finest filigreed gold, set with seed pearls and diamonds. As it lay on the floor of the basement room, amid the stench of gunpowder, the red enamel of the boyar's coat was matched in hue by the steady drip-drip of thin Romanov blood that soon covered the steadfast quartz soldier. . . .

New York

1

"*Avez-vous quelque chose à déclarer, Mademoiselle Fein?*" asked the customs official as he glanced at my passport. I shifted uncomfortably as I leaned over the baggage inspection counter. Perhaps because of the way I was raised, I've never been able to lie and feel right about it. And now I was going to have to lie. The official repeated his question, this time in English. "Do you have anything to declare, Mademoiselle Fein?"

"No, nothing," I lied, and suddenly remembering my instructions, I hurriedly added, "Except my good intentions." The customs man smiled broadly as I gave the proper passwords. To make sure I'd gone to the proper guard, I awaited the countersign. Sure enough, he gave it. "Paris is the City of Lights," he said. "I am sure you will enjoy your holiday here."

As the customs guard spoke, he put X marks in chalk and some official stickers on all my brand-new Gucci luggage, and waved me through the balance of the customs procedures at De Gaulle airport, just outside Paris.

I sighed inwardly in relief. The guard hadn't asked me to open the matching Gucci handbag I carried slung over my shoulder. Inside the handbag was a small package I was to deliver to a man I had never seen, in three days' time. As to what was inside the package I carried—well, I just didn't know. I wasn't supposed to know, either. I was acting only as a courier.

You could well wonder how a young woman of eighteen from a small town in Southern California found herself playing foreign intrigue games at the Paris airport. I don't blame you; I often wonder about it myself. Oh, I almost forgot to mention it. I am a secret agent in the employ of an equally secret agency of your government and mine. Yep, that's right: a spy, a spook, a cloak-and-dagger type.

How it happened? Well, I promise you that I didn't answer an ad in *The New York Times* for Spy Wanted. I sort of stumbled into becoming a spy, and in the process I was kidnapped, manhandled, and nearly done in by a notorious paid killer. I still get an occasional shudder when I think about how close I came to being the late Doris Fein!

As I entered the passenger terminal at De Gaulle, I felt as though I'd suddenly been dropped into some future time. Most airports look alike and, except for the signs being in different languages, you could be almost anywhere in the world. But not De Gaulle. It's extremely futuristic. I half expected to see Captain Kirk or Mr. Spock at any minute.

I spotted the exit that led to where I could get a cab to Paris. It wasn't all that hard. The word for cab in French is the same as in English: *taxi*. Now, I would have to find a specific cab and driver, according to the instructions I'd received in New York, just two days before. My orders had come from George Case, my boss—actually, everyone's boss in the Organization. His official title is Director of Operations, and it was George Case who first put me on Uncle Sam's payroll.

I'm sure you saw on TV or read in the newspapers about the short, ill-fated revolution in the African nation of Dakama. It lasted only a few days, but was so well covered by the media, probably everyone in the world knew about it. "Film at eleven" as they say. One day, I'll be watching something on TV, and there'll be an interruption by the network news department. A newsperson will come on and say: "Today the world came to an end . . . film at eleven." But back to the Dakaman uprising.

It just so happens that my Aunt Lois, my mother's sister, is married to a very important man in Dakama's affairs. His name is Claude Bernard, and he's the American economic attaché to the Dakaman mission at the UN. When the revolution began, it was to have been coordinated with terrorist attacks on the UN staff in New York. The revolutionaries tried to kidnap my aunt and uncle. The attempt failed, but the Intelligence Gathering Organization (IGO) spirited them both away for safekeeping after that. The IGO is the outfit I spy for, but not then, I didn't.

Just as all this was going on, I arrived in New York City for my first vacation as a solo, adult person. I'd graduated with highest honors from Santa Amelia High, in my hometown of Santa Amelia, California. As a reward, my parents had arranged for me to stay with my aunt and uncle in New York for six weeks.

But when I arrived in New York, I saw my uncle for only a few minutes. In the excitement of the revolution, my aunt and uncle had forgotten completely that I was due to visit them. I got to their apartment just as Uncle Claude was packing. In the space of a few minutes, I was shifted from my relatives' apartment to a suite at the Plaza Hotel. That didn't anger me; I adore the Plaza. But then, my aunt and uncle vanished utterly!

Fearing that they'd been victims of foul play, as the newscasters say, I went to the New York City Police Department. No one at the police station I went to believed me or my story. Or even cared. The UN people aren't under the jurisdiction of the city police. They have diplomatic immunity. But one detective, a very handsome man named Carl Suzuki, believed me. Together, we tried to locate my missing relatives. In the process, I was kidnapped myself, got hired as an agent by the IGO to help find my aunt and uncle and, as I say, nearly murdered by the terrorists.

At the last moment, the IGO came to my rescue. Which isn't to say that I was sitting about, praying for deliverance at the time. I had just about escaped from my captors by the time the IGO got around to me. It turned out my aunt and uncle were still alive.

The whole affair was strictly hush-hush, as the IGO isn't allowed to operate inside the continental United States.

Once my part in the affair was over, George Case, the director of the IGO, put me on the payroll to guarantee my silence. I was paid a year's salary in advance (a sizable sum) and told that if I broke security and talked about the Dakaman affair, I would be subject to disciplinary action within the IGO. So as I said, I wasn't really a working secret agent. I was being paid to keep my mouth shut.

Although I hadn't been harmed physically, the entire Dakaman affair had made a shambles out of my personal life. You see, the danger and excitement of the investigation brought Carl Suzuki and me very, very close emotionally. In fact, just as I was about to get physically involved with Carl, something I had never done with anyone, my childhood sweetheart, Larry Small, showed up in New York.

Larry had seen the news reports about Dakama and knew about my family connections. Frightened and concerned for my safety, he had borrowed air fare from a friend of ours and, with him, had flown to New York. He arrived at the Plaza just as I had made my decision about Carl Suzuki. Carl and I had walked into the lobby of the Plaza, arm in arm, only to be greeted by a very angry, very jealous Larry Small! After that, needless to say, nothing ever happened between Carl and me.

And that's what really burns me. You see, there

never had been anything physical between Larry and me, other than some heavy necking. But the way Larry acted toward Carl Suzuki indicated otherwise. I resented it like mad. No one owns Doris Fein but Ms. Fein, thank you!

But Carl is a Japanese-American. Third generation born in this country. In some ways, he's no more Japanese than McDonald's. In others, he's as stiff-necked and honor-bound as any samurai swordsman. Respecting what he thought was another man's woman, Carl did a fast fadeout, and I was minus one admirer. I was absolutely furious at both Larry and Carl! In a short time, Larry had to get back to his job in California and took off. But Carl still didn't try to get in touch with me. To make matters even drearier, my parents showed up in New York and checked into my hotel, the Plaza.

They had been enjoying their first vacation together since I was born. Dad had been attending a medical convention in Hawaii with Mom when the news about Dakama broke. They were concerned for both me and my aunt and uncle and grabbed the first flight to New York. They arrived shortly after all the shouting and shooting had ended, but right on time to ruin my solo vacation in New York! I once heard a TV comedian make a crack about taking one's mother-in-law on a honeymoon. That's about how I felt. There I was, installed in my own suite at one of the most elegant hostelries in the world. I had a government check for twenty thousand dollars: my hush

money. I had a new wardrobe for my trip and, outside of my parents, no one to see me wear it. For
good measure, Mom and Dad insisted on making the
remainder of my vacation a family affair.

Make no mistake. I adore my parents. They are the
most wonderful and understanding couple any girl
could wish for. My dad is an ophthalmologist and
Mom was his nurse for years. They are bright, witty,
attractive people. But they *are* my parents, and darn
it, it was my vacation they were spoiling! I was torn
between annoyance at them and remembering how
much I owed them for all they've done for me. For
as long as I can recall, my folks have been one hundred percent supportive of me in everything I've
done. And I *have* enjoyed both privileges and posses-
sions. They even bought a car for me in my senior
year in Santa Amelia High. It's my darling gumdrop
car, a lime-green Triumph sports car that looks like
it's going a hundred miles an hour even when it's
standing still.

But for every privilege I've been given by my parents, I have accepted responsibilities as well. I've
made it a point to excel at my schoolwork and
worked as Dad's receptionist during summer vaca-
tions. I think being Dad's receptionist gave me valuable experience in learning about people and their
problems. I think, too, responsibilities when you're
young make you a better person as an adult. As Dad
put it to me when he bought me the flying gumdrop:
"Dee-Dee," he said (he calls me that, I'm afraid),

"there is no magic to the age of eighteen years. No one will wave a fairy wand and say that you are now a full-fledged adult person. Being a mature person starts much earlier. That way, by the time you get to voting age, you've already become an adult."

I've always done my best to live up to my parents' expectations. In fact, the only thing in which I may have disappointed my mother is my weight problem. Oh, not that I have to go through doors sideways, or anything like that, but I must confess that a sylph I am not. I've looked on in envy all my life at those people who can eat anything at all and stay maddeningly skinny. I just *look* at a bread stick and I gain a pound! Grandmother Fein says that I'm *zoftig,* which is a nice Yiddish way of saying voluptuous, but I've never believed it. Grandma tries to make me feel better about the way I look.

Face it, I live in Southern California, where the standards of beauty are different from anywhere else on earth. Back home, a good-looking girl is tall, slim, blonde, and vaguely resembles a Barbie doll. And there seem to be so many girls back home who look like that! I, on the other hand, am five feet four inches tall, have brown hair and hazel eyes and, by California standards, weigh about fifteen pounds more than I should. But I have great teeth; they're my best feature. They should be. My Uncle Saul Fein is a dentist. From the time I cut my second teeth to about two years ago, I walked around with so much dental silver in my mouth, you could have melted it down and made a service for six in sterling. I guess it was during the braces-on-the-teeth time that Petunia began to take over my personality.

I should explain that Petunia is my alter ego. Doris Fein is basically a sensible, slightly overweight person. But Petunia Fein is a person for whom a pint of Baskin-Robbins ice cream is a casual snack before a pepperoni and cheese pizza. During my metal-in-the-mouth days, I used to see handsome, intelligent boys and wish with all my heart that they'd notice me. And each time that they'd go off with a Barbie doll, Petunia would take over.

By the time my overeating was recognized as a real problem, and Mom and I talked it out, I had ballooned to wearing half sizes from the Ladies' Dress Department. I was all of fifteen. Once I realized deep down that I was eating to cover up a hurt, controlling my weight became easier. I do have lapses from time to time, but I've dropped enough weight over the past three years so that I no longer resemble a medicine ball in a print dress. But I don't think I'll ever really be thin.

That's why I was so enchanted with the attention paid to me by Carl Suzuki. He didn't think I was fat. He thought I was *zoftig*. He told me that many Japanese men prefer a full-bodied woman. I nearly grabbed the first plane for Tokyo!

But darn Larry Small! He had chased off the first intelligent, handsome man I'd met who thought of me as sexy. I'm used to being praised for my mind and my scholastic accomplishments. I've been a straight A student all my life. And why not? I didn't have all those tall, muscular surfer types distracting me with their amorous attentions. Studying was as easy as eating.

So there I sat in my Plaza suite with a large sum of money, a great wardrobe, and no one with whom to share it, except for my parents. In a word, I was B-O-R-E-D. That's when I decided I would go to France. After all, I'm of age, and if my folks felt me responsible enough to solo-vacation it in New York, why not Paris?

They took it well. Dad was terribly concerned at first until Uncle Claude assured him that he would see I was looked after by some of his higher-up diplomatic friends in Paris. He's very well connected. I also think my parents were relieved that they could spend the rest of their interrupted vacation alone. They haven't been to New York since their honeymoon. But just as I was about to call Pan-Am for a reservation, I remembered something important. When I took the money from George Case and the IGO, I was told that I had to check with the organization before I left the country. I already had my passport. My dad had suggested I get it for ID purposes. There are places in the USA where a driver's license isn't enough positive identification. So I was all set, except I needed permission from my "employer," the IGO, to leave.

I rummaged among my papers, looking for the

telephone number I'd been given by George Case, on the chance I would need to contact him. After all, when you want to call a secret agency, you don't just look in the Yellow Pages under Spies. I found the number. It was a local New York exchange and area code. I knew this had to be a blind, as the headquarters for the IGO are somewhere in Maryland, just outside Washington, D.C.

I dialed the number and after three rings, a man's voice said, "Six-oh-two-five."

"I want to speak with George Case," I said.

"I'm sorry. We have no such person at this number," said the voice.

"That can't be," I protested. "He gave me this number himself."

"Who is this calling?"

"My name is Doris Fein. Mr. Case knows me. I'm staying at the Plaza Hotel."

"I'm sorry, Miss Fein," said the man's voice. "But this is the Old World Trading Corporation in Brooklyn. We have no person of that name on our staff. You must have a wrong number."

Before I could say anything else, there was a dry click, and I found myself looking at a dead phone. Puzzled, I hung up. I walked over to the window of my suite that faced the Pulitzer Fountain and watched the hansom cabs go in and out of Central Park. I was still wondering how to reach George Case when the telephone rang.

"Doris Fein here," I said.

"Listen carefully and follow these instructions to the letter," said a woman's voice, without any preamble. "At six fifteen this evening, go out from your hotel to the hansom cab lineup near the fountain—"

"Just a moment," I cut in. "Who is this? Who are you?"

"Take the first hansom cab in the line," said the woman's voice, as though I hadn't interrupted her. "The driver will be a middle-aged blonde woman, wearing a vest and a yellow plastic rose in the band of her top hat—"

"I am going nowhere and doing nothing until I know who this is, and what this is about," I interjected firmly. I heard a sound on the line that could have been a sigh of impatience. Then a voice I recognized came on.

"Dammit, Ms. Fein," said George Case, "are you incapable of following even a simple set of orders without causing a fuss? And *please* don't mention my name on this line if you recognize my voice!"

"Recognize it?" I said. "I'll never forget it!"

"Then follow instructions, just once, won't you?" said Case angrily. "Do as you're told, and contact with you will be made. Understood?"

"Understood," I said dutifully. The woman's voice came back on the line then, and she began repeating her instructions. I wrote it all down on the telephone table note pad up till the point where she said, "Do *not* write these instructions down, Ms. Fein. If you have already done so, destroy the paper. If you have written these instructions on a note pad, also destroy the three pages underneath the page you have used."

I glanced down at the note pad I had used, then looked all around the room. Silly, I guess. But when the voice mentioned the note pad, I suddenly felt as though somehow, some way, I was being watched, even as I spoke on the telephone. The woman on the other end didn't wait for me to acknowledge her message. She hung up.

Obediently, at exactly six fifteen that evening, I left the side entrance to the Plaza and walked directly to the hansom cab stand opposite. As promised, the driver was a woman who fitted the description given to me over the phone. I climbed into the cab. Without a word, the driver urged the horse into motion and we swung into Central Park.

There's a charming, scenic drive that follows the inner circumference of Central Park. The charm is somewhat mitigated by the fact that the drive is shared by horse-drawn and motor vehicles. On certain days, I've been told, the park drive is closed to autos. Unhappily, this wasn't one of the days. By the time we came to a traffic light at 79th Street near the Metropolitan Museum, I'm sure I'd absorbed a double lungful of carbon monoxide fumes. New York pollution standards for cars are nowhere as strict as California's. Sometimes you feel as though you could *chew* the air in the Big Apple, as they call it.

As we waited at the traffic light, a big black Lincoln limousine slid up alongside us. I noticed immediately that all the glass except for its windshield was tinted so darkly that one couldn't see inside. The rear window on the side nearest me slipped silkily down, and I found myself looking right into the face of George Case. He opened the door and called out.

"Get in quickly! The light's about to change!"

I scrambled down from the hansom cab and, just before the traffic light turned green, got inside the big Lincoln. But not before a taxicab behind us at the signal began tooting his horn. We pulled away swiftly from the light as George Case said to me, "You know, I once heard a split second defined as the time it takes between when the light turns green and the idiot behind you starts honking."

"I've heard that said," I replied, looking directly at George Case as I spoke. I didn't like this man; never had. The ruthless way in which he and his organization worked was very off-putting. I was about to launch into the reason I had telephoned the IGO when a radio phone in the back seat began to buzz. Case picked up the phone and growled into it, "Hold this, and all other calls. I'm with uncleared personnel, dammit!" Then he hung up and turned to me. "Well, Ms. Fein," he said ungraciously, "what's your problem now?"

"No problem," I said. "Just following instructions. I want to go to Paris, and according to our agreement, I need permission. That's why I called."

"Paris! Really?" said George Case, smiling. Actually, I should say showing his teeth. There was neither humor nor warmth to the way he had arranged his features. "I'm surprised," he continued. "I thought you loved New York. Or has something gone wrong between you and your Oriental boyfriend, Ms. Fein?"

"Not at all," I lied. "It's just that I've always wanted to see Paris. Now that I have the money, courtesy of the IGO, I'm going to go there. That is, if it's all right with the IGO."

"Now, this is very interesting, Ms. Fein," said Case, showing more teeth. "Because if you hadn't contacted me, I would have been in touch with you very soon. . . ."

"I won't give back the twenty thousand, if that's what you're after," I said shortly. "It's mine and I earned it, putting my life on the line. I suppose now that the Dakaman revolution has fizzled, you want your hush money back. You figure that what I know about it doesn't matter anymore. Is that it?"

"If you'd stop attacking me and listen to what I have to say, you might find out," said Case heatedly. "And as to the money, it's yours. Irrevocably. I represent a perfectly legitimate agency of your government. You were promised that money. It's yours. Would your government go back on its word or break a promise?"

"You should ask that question of any American

Indian tribe our honorable government ever made a treaty with," I responded. "And I think you'll get the same answer."

"That's not fair, Ms. Fein," Case replied, feigning offense. "I am not with the Department of Indian Affairs. I am with the IGO."

"Ooooh," I said, elaborately. "That's a different matter! Wasn't it the IGO that assured me I was in no danger acting as a decoy during the Dakaman affair?" I noted Case's look of discomfort with inner satisfaction. "As I recall," I continued, "I got *that* promise from the IGO shortly before I was kidnapped and nearly murdered by terrorists. Sure, I trust your promises, Mr. Case. As far as I can throw this limousine!"

"That was a different matter, Ms. Fein," Case soothed. "We did our damndest to protect you. It was an unfortunate set of unavoidable circumstances that put you in jeopardy. But we did get you out of trouble, didn't we?"

"I was already halfway out of my trouble when your people finally showed up," I said bitterly. "And I did it all by myself. If I'd have waited for you and the US Cavalry to arrive, I would have been long dead and gone!"

"I won't bandy words with you, Ms. Fein," Case said. "Say what you will, you were protected. And we saved your life that night on the George Washington Bridge. You were rolling all over the roadway up there with your anatomy hanging out when my men rescued you. If you were in command of that situation, it sure didn't look like it to me!"

I felt my face grow warm. Some of what Case said was true. I had been captive in an ambulance, on my way to an unmarked grave somewhere in suburban New Jersey when the IGO blockaded the bridge exit. And my captor was indeed an internationally notorious political assassin, masquerading as a doctor.

But far from sitting and awaiting my fate, I was trying to escape when the blockade caused the ambulance to make an abrupt U turn on the bridge. I had opened the back doors of the ambulance and was about to jump out. My would-be executioner had grabbed at my clothing when I jumped from the back of the moving vehicle. The clothing stayed in his clutches, but I didn't. My dress tore, and I rolled out onto the roadway of the George Washington Bridge wearing panty hose, shoes, and nothing else but a terrified expression! I don't wear a bra, and the weather had been too warm for any other undergarments. But evidently, it would be some time before I'd be allowed to forget my impromptu topless performance on the bridge.

"I'll give you a point or two there," I said grudgingly to George Case. "But I was already free when your men showed up."

"Whatever," said Case, waving a hand impatiently. "But getting back to your request for travel. If Paris is where you want to go, I see no reason why not. In fact, if you'll meet me at your hotel for dinner at"—

he consulted the Rolex Oyster on his wrist—"ten o'clock, I may have an interesting business proposition for you."

"I will be having dinner with my parents at nine," I said coolly. "And I see no reason to change my plans. I don't trust your propositions, Mr. Case. The way it is, I count myself as lucky to be alive."

"Have it your own way, Ms. Fein." Case shrugged. "I just thought that you might enjoy your Parisian vacation more if it didn't cost you a dime of your twenty thousand dollars from us. You see, I can offer you a way to see Paris in utter luxury. And Uncle Sam will pick up the tab." Case sat back in the cushy upholstery of the car and fell silent.

And that's where I made my crucial mistake. I may have conquered Petunia's appetite for food, but greed can take many forms. So, in retrospect, I have no one to blame but myself for what happened afterwards. I said to George Case, "I'll meet you *after* dinner, at the Oak Room bar."

"You won't regret this decision," George Case said, making the most gross misstatement one human being has ever made to another. "You won't regret it a bit!"

2

"I'll be honest with you, Ms. Fein," said George Case. "It's an important job, but your part in it will be minor. You will only have to deliver a package."

"Containing what?" I asked.

"An object of value to our cause," Case replied.

"No deal, for two reasons," I said. "First, you said you were going to be honest with me. You never have been in the past, and now you want to make a special point of telling me you're being honest. That means I'm being lied to." Case began to protest, but I said, "Please, let me finish. The second reason is that I won't know the contents of the package. For all I know, I could be transporting something that could get me jailed by French authorities. I mean, I saw *Midnight Express.*"

"I can personally guarantee that you won't be carrying drugs, or any contraband substance. In fact, we have the full cooperation of the French Sûreté in this matter. You won't even have to open your luggage going through French customs. How's that for a guarantee?"

"Right here, in the Oak Room," I said, indicating our surroundings at the posh bar in the Plaza Hotel, "it sounds great. But what good is your guarantee if the French ship me off to Devil's Island?"

"Devil's Island has been shut down as a penal colony for the French government for years," Case said heavily. "The last I heard, someone was going to build a resort hotel on the island."

"Well, you know what I mean," I said. "I don't want to end up any place the French ship their smugglers off to."

"You will be acting as a courier, not a smuggler." Case sighed. "And if we have the cooperation of the French . . . well, you can't smuggle something into a country when the government says it's perfectly all right to bring it in."

"Swell," I said. "Let me see that in writing from the French."

"Oh, really, Ms. Fein," Case said. "We *are* a secret agency, you know. And this sort of international cooperation is definitely on a hush-hush basis."

"Let me get this straight," I said. "All I must do is carry a small package in my handbag through French customs, who will look the other way. I then will hold on to the package for three days, and deliver it to a man in Paris. But I won't know what's in the package, nor what happens to it once I've turned it over to the man in Paris. Right?"

"Exactly, so far," Case said.

"And in exchange for this service, I get all my expenses and travel paid for. I can stay in France for as long as my vacation lasts, and all that I spend is chargeable to the IGO, right again?"

"Right."

I toyed with my glass of Perrier water and thought a bit. The last time I trusted this man, he nearly got me killed. But this proposition seemed harmless enough. Then I saw the obvious hole in the logic of what Case was offering to me!

"Why me?" I asked. "Surely, if this is such a routine matter, you have many people in your employ who could deliver this package. And never have any curiosity about what's in it. Why should you pay for my vacation, when somebody already on the payroll could do this job? I'm beginning to smell a mouse, if not a large rat, Mr. Case."

"All right, all right, you've got me there, Ms. Fein," said Case ruefully. "The reason we picked you is that you're not known to any foreign operatives as an agent of ours. But don't you see? That's another guarantee of your safety. No one is looking for you, no one suspects you could be an IGO agent—"

"Including me," I put in. "Because I'm not an agent and never was."

"On the contrary, Ms. Fein," Case oiled. "By contract, and you have signed one and accepted our check, you *are* an agent of the IGO."

"Are we back to the money again?" I asked. "I've told you, I consider the check I got as money earned. I owe you and the IGO nothing!"

"Nobody's saying you do," Case replied. "If we thought that, why should we offer you an all-expense-paid luxury European vacation for this simple dropoff of a parcel?"

"Exactly the point I'm making," I said. "There has to be more to it."

"Oh, all right." Case sighed resignedly. "I'll tell you the story. But first, what do you know about agriculture?"

"You put the seeds in the ground and water them," I said. "And after a while pansies grow." It may have sounded facetious, but my mother's flower garden had been my sole connection with growing anything in my entire life.

"Then this may take a while," said Case, motioning to a waiter for a refill of his Scotch and water. I indicated that I was fine with my undrunk Perrier. "As you know, from the newspapers," Case explained, "population has grown tremendously all over the world since the end of World War II. The energy crisis is nothing compared to the crisis that will arise by the year 2000. Unless something is done in the next few years, we can expect to see over half the world's population starving to death."

I nodded agreement. I'd read a great deal about this. In his passion for growth and his heedless plundering of our natural resources, man was going to become extinct by starvation in the next few generations. Unless, of course, he blew himself to atoms before that.

Case continued his explanation. "Feeding the world will be the major problem of the twenty-first century. Our scientists and the specialists in the Soviet and Chinese blocs have been doing research on a crash priority basis for the past five years. And I'm delighted and proud to say, it's been the USA that has come up with the solution." He reached into his coat pocket and took out a manila envelope, folded over once. He handed it to me, saying, "Go ahead, you can open it."

The envelope contained photographs of some particularly barren landscape. Off in the far distance, across snow-covered ground, I could make out a mountain range. Outside of that, it was an ordinary photo of a winter scene.

"That picture was taken in Idaho last November," Case said. "Now look at the next picture."

The next shot was taken from exactly the same vantage point as the previous bleak landscape. But through the snow on the ground, I could see a remarkable thing. There was something growing up through the white blanket of snow and, when the photo had been taken, whatever was growing had reached a height of about three feet!

"The second picture was taken in February of this year," Case said. "Amazing, isn't it?"

"It would be, if I knew what we were talking about," I replied.

"Oh yeah," Case said. "You only know from pansies. Well, Ms. Fein, what you see growing there is wheat. It was planted in November."

"I've heard about winter wheat," I said.

"Then you know that it's planted late in the year,

and it grows in spring," Case said. "In some northern climates, the ground is still too frozen to plow and plant in the early spring. Planting is done before the first snow flies, and then in the spring, when the ground thaws, the seeds sprout and come up."

"And this is connected somehow to this trip you want me to take?" I asked.

"It surely is, Ms. Fein," Case said. "You evidently don't get the implication of these two photos. The wheat you see growing is coming up through the snow in *February.* By spring, it will be tall enough to be harvested! Don't you see? This is true winter wheat. It will grow even in snow and below-freezing temperatures. It means the land can produce food crops all year round! It can mean an end to starving millions during the time when crops can't be grown!"

I sat back in my chair. If I could whistle, which I can't, I would have. This was important, and important to all of humanity!

"And the wheat is just the beginning of it, Ms. Fein," Case continued with enthusiasm. "Our labs are now on the verge of being able to do the same thing with staple crops other than wheat. It all came out of enzyme research during the Vietnamese war."

"You mean something good came of it?" I asked in wonder.

"I must admit, it was accidental," Case conceded. "Our labs were looking for a defoliating agent that wouldn't have the poisonous, long-term effects of dioxin—what the press calls Agent Orange."

"You mean the stuff that's still killing our own soldiers who sprayed it in Vietnam?" I asked.

"There has been no definite link established between Agent Orange and cancer in Vietnamese war veterans," Case said stiffly. "But in any event, our labs were working on a substance that would simply make plants *think* that it was time to stop growing. An enzyme just like the substances manufactured by the plants themselves. Enzymes make plants grow. Ergo, an enzyme could be developed that would make them *not* grow. We never did find an anti-growth enzyme. But what we found is a million times better. A small, a *minute* amount of this stuff, applied to *any* seed crop, makes it grow. Under any conditions, regardless of climate."

"You mean this enzyme could make oranges grow in Maine?" I asked.

"It's not that good," Case said. "But when applied to certain crops already nurtured for hardiness, as winter wheat is, not only does it grow in adverse conditions, but the enzyme seems to double or treble its inherent hardiness."

"That's wonderful!" I said. "You're right. It can mean an end to starvation!" Then I thought for a second. "But what has this to do with my European trip?"

"Well, Ms. Fein, I am not allowed to tell you just what is in the parcel you'll be carrying to France. But what if . . . and I stress the 'if' . . . what if you were transporting a sample of this enzyme to secret French laboratories?"

"It would make all the difference in the world," I said quickly. "But explain something. Why should all this be kept a secret? A discovery like this should be given to the entire world!"

"I'm not the humanitarian that you are, Ms. Fein," Case said. "I am a security man. It's been mentioned in certain quarters that if a nation like Red China had this enzyme, it would be able to support even more population than it does now. And as it stands, the Red Chinese can field the largest army the world has ever known. Can you imagine the size of their land force if they could count on unlimited population, all well fed on year-round crops of rice?"

I let the question go unanswered. Case's implication was plain. "But why an actual sample of the enzyme?" I asked. "Couldn't you just send the formula?"

"Policy," Case answered. "We've spent billions on this project secretly. And even though we love our allies, we aren't about to hand out for free the proceeds of five years of research. Our diplomatic corps wants a lot more than a thank you from our allies. On top of which, they don't believe the stuff does what it's supposed to do without testing it themselves."

"I see," I said. "And I'll be transporting the sample."

"I didn't say that," Case said quickly. "If you were, I still couldn't say that. A courier operates on a need-to-know basis. But as you are one of the more unusual of our operatives . . ."

"Meaning I won't do it unless I know what it's about," I said.

"And in view of the fact that all secrets can't last long with electronic surveillance being what it is," Case said, "you can be a perfect courier for us. No one alive knows you're on our payroll. You're younger by far than anyone we've ever used, and you are already on a well-established-in-fact vacation. You're ideal for this one assignment."

"It sounds innocent enough. . . ."

"Because it *is* innocent," Case put in. "You'll be helping your government and, in doing so, be helping the whole population of the planet. *If* that is what the parcel contains. And understand, I am admitting nothing. Do we have a deal?"

I thought for a second longer, then extended my hand to George Case across the table. "I'll buy myself a trench coat and dark glasses today," I said. "When do I leave?"

"One thing at a time," Case said. "First, forget the trench coat. You are to travel first class, with all the trimmings and trappings of a wealthy American tourist. I suggest that you go shopping for a smart wardrobe and some matching luggage." He took a piece of paper from his pocket. "But make sure you buy your luggage at Gucci's. Here's the specific style number. Buy all but the shoulder bag. A special bag with a compartment for the parcel has already been made up. The rest of your luggage must match it."

"And how do I pay for all this?" I asked. "Out of the money I've already received from the IGO?" I asked merely as a formality. Now that I knew I was doing something really useful to all the world, I didn't care about the money. If what Case told me was so, I'd have gladly given every cent. Imagine—knowing that I, Doris Fein, could be instrumental in eliminating starvation in the world! But Case waved his hand airily.

"An envelope containing five thousand dollars in traveler's checks will be delivered by hand to you in your suite tomorrow morning at ten," he said. "Your airline ticket is already paid for, and you can pick up your ticket at the airport on Friday, just before you leave. Flight information and arrival times will be in the same package with your traveler's checks."

"But Friday is only the day after tomorrow," I protested. "I have a million things to do before I can leave."

"How many people can starve in one day, Ms. Fein?" asked Case. "Each day we delay the trip is one day lost before we can get this project going. Just shop quickly for what you need, that's all." Case motioned to the waiter again and called for the bill.

"You were pretty sure I was going to take this assignment, weren't you?" I asked.

Case fidgeted for a second. "Not at all," he said easily. "But against the chance you did, we were ready to roll. As I said, time is vital." He paid the bill when the waiter brought it and, oddly enough, Case gave me a courtly little bow as he stood up to leave. "Good luck, and enjoy your vacation, Ms. Fein," he said.

I was so taken by the sudden show of courtesy and concern, I softened a bit toward Case. "You can call me Doris," I said.

"And you may call me Mr. Case," he replied. "Never forget that you work for the IGO. And I am its director. Good night . . . Doris."

He turned abruptly and walked to the exit door that led to the Plaza lobby, a balding, slightly pudgy man, rumpled about the edges and wearing a worried look. He looked more like a tired businessman in from Buffalo than the head of one of the most powerful secret agencies in the world.

The next morning, just after I'd stepped out of my shower, I caught a glimpse of the chambermaid as she was finishing up in the living room of my suite at the Plaza. She smiled and waved cheerily as she closed the door to the outside corridor.

I looked at my bedroom. The bed wasn't made and, having been in the shower when the maid had arrived, I knew that I hadn't been given fresh towels. *Very* un-Plaza-like service. I was about to go after her, or call the housekeeping department of the hotel, when I noticed the Gucci shoulder bag on the couch in my sitting room. I quickly crossed the room and opened the bag.

It had my initials on the side and inside was a bulky envelope containing my traveler's checks. I could also feel, through the lining of the bag, a small parcel somehow sewn inside. It couldn't have been more than five by three inches. I opened the envelope and found a small, typewritten note headed: *Destroy after reading.* It read:

After arriving at De Gaulle airport, you will go through customs. When asked by the official if you have anything to declare, you will reply: "Nothing except my good intentions." The customs official will reply: "Paris is the City of Lights. I am sure you will enjoy your holiday here." He will then pass your baggage through without inspection. You will proceed by taxicab to the Hotel Henri IV at 31 avenue George V, just off the Champs Elysées. Accommodations of top quality are arranged for you effective your arrival date.

Once you are safely and completely alone in your suite, you will press the two brass studs located in the bottom of your shoulder bag, provided by the Organization. This will release the parcel. You will then uncover the flush tank lid in your bathroom and drop the parcel inside until it is time to deliver same. Particulars about delivery procedures will be given to you by telephone after arrival. The caller will identify himself by giving the password: "Demeter." Your countersign is "Ceres." End message.

As I burned the message and dropped it down the bathroom convenience, I thought to myself, "Well, no doubt about it, Doris Fein. You are now a full-fledged secret agent!"

Paris

3

I fought my way through the small army of "genuine English-speaking guides" that lined the approach to the taxicab exit. My porter carried my baggage to the first cab in the line and, in hardly any time at all, I was on my way to Paris. I suppose that somebody does stay at the several first-class hotels near the airport; they have a ubiquitous Holiday Inn and a few names that sound particularly unappetizing.

My driver, unlike the New York cabbies I'd become accustomed to, was silent as a mime troupe throughout the drive. Too bad. It was my first view of Paris and environs, and I had no one to ooh and ahh about things with. I felt like the story of the rabbi playing golf on Yom Kippur. He hits a hole-in-one, but whom can he tell?

De Gaulle airport lies outside Paris, about ten miles from the city. Coming in to Paris proper, you pass through the north of the city. I was taken by the way the Parisians have dealt with new construction. For the most part, the new structures are the same height as the old, and the view one gets of Paris is an odd juxtaposition of modern and traditional. At first, the cab ride took us past more new buildings than old. Then, there it was . . . the Eiffel Tower. I could see it in the distance looming above the rooftops.

Every famous city has at least one building or area uniquely its own: something that says to the world, "This is New York," or, "This is San Francisco"—a trademark, if you will. Paris seems to have more than its share. I had just thought, "The Eiffel Tower. This is truly Paris," when we made our way toward the center of the city and, for the first time outside of movies or books, I saw the Arch of Triumph. Again I said, "This is Paris"—until we passed the famous arch and I saw the Champs Elysées, the Fifth Avenue of Paris. . . . Well, I almost dislocated my neck trying to see as much as I could.

But when we pulled up in front of the Hotel Henri IV and I was shown into the lobby, that was it. If the Henri IV isn't the typification of a luxury Paris hotel, I don't know what is. The doorman looked like a Russian admiral in service to the tsar. The entire hotel is decorated in the style of the 1700s, and as I went through the check-in process, I chanced to look at a clock on a nearby wall. I suddenly realized that the timepiece wasn't a reproduction of an eighteenth century ormolu clock. It was the real thing!

The service was beyond belief. I don't know if it was the fact that the IGO had specified only first-class accommodations, or if the hotel treats everyone who stays there that way, but in a short time, I felt like the last dowager empress of China. They say that she was so haughty that she never looked around her when she decided to sit down. She merely sat down, knowing that someone would automatically push a chair between her and the floor.

It wasn't until I'd been shown to my room and tipped the bellperson that I realized something. I had been in France for over two hours and, outside of the cabbie, I hadn't spoken a word of French to anyone. I studied French for four years in high school, and I'd been looking forward to using it. But each time I'd been about to use my French, I discovered that virtually all the help at the Henri IV spoke better English than I did French.

I didn't even bother to unpack. I wanted to be out and doing, seeing Paris. After satisfying myself that my suite at the hotel was suitable for at least a countess, I carried my Gucci shoulder bag into the bathroom of the suite.

I did a double take when I entered the john. No, it wasn't the oversized bathtub and the simply *yards* of ultrathick towels. Nor was it the hand-held shower head that coiled like a wall telephone against the inside of the tub enclosure. It was a porcelain convenience right near the john itself. For a crazy minute I thought a mistake had been made in planning the room. There were *two* johns!

Then, as I looked closer at the second convenience, I realized what it was: a bidet. I'd heard of bidets, but had never seen one. If you've never heard of a bidet, the Twentieth-Century Webster defines it as a "low porcelain bowl-shaped bathroom fixture, equipped with running water, used for bathing the crotch."

Not an elegant definition, but an accurate description nonetheless. For the umpteenth time in a few hours, I looked at something and said, "This is *really* Paris!"

I pressed the two studs on the bag and, as though spring-loaded, the small parcel inside the lining popped out into the interior of the bag. It was wrapped in a plastic, waterproof substance that sealed it much like a boil-in-the-bag portion of broccoli in butter sauce. So carefully sealed was the package that any ideas of my taking a peek at the contents were out of the question.

The john fixture itself posed something of a problem, if I was to hide the parcel as instructed. My main problem was getting it into the flush tank of the john. It wasn't the low, lever-action water tank one is accustomed to in the United States. This water tank was one of those old-fashioned gravity types, with the flush box high on the wall above the john and a connecting pipe that ran down five feet to join the porcelain part. In order to get the package inside, I had to stand on the seat of the john on my tiptoes to reach the upper edge of the flush box.

I had just managed to get the darned package inside the box and was teetering on the edge of the john seat when there was a knock at my door, from the outside corridor. I wasn't expecting anyone and, in my haste to go and answer the door, I'm afraid that my foot slipped getting down from the john seat. In the space of a second, I found myself still standing, despite the fall. But although one of my feet was on solid tile bathroom floor, the other was planted firmly inside the john bowl with water up to my ankle!

Soggily, I went to the outside door of my suite and opened it. Standing there with a bemused look on his face was a room service waiter with a cart. On the cart were a bottle of champagne and a basket of fruit, all trimmed with flowers. If the waiter noticed my sopping wet left foot and the dark moist footprints that led from the john, he said nothing. Not a smile, not a smirk. I've heard it said that the employees of Paris hotels are the very souls of discretion. To my everlasting gratitude, it's so.

The waiter rolled the cart with fruit, flowers, and wine to a beautiful gilt table and chair set up near a window that overlooked the avenue George V. He agitated the champagne in the cooler, which I swear was silver, and said, *"Voilà, mademoiselle.* Compliments of the management." While I was debating with myself whether this service would require a tip (I'd been warned that *everything* does in Paris), the waiter smiled again and almost bowed his way out of my suite.

I went over and inspected the gift from the hotel management. I nearly fell through the floor when I saw the label on the champagne. It was Dom Perignon. Never mind what year; there are no cheap years when it comes to Dom Perignon. It was then that I saw a small white card amid the flowers. I picked it up casually, expecting to see some message of welcome from the management. But instead it read: *Remain in room for the next two hours. Expect your phone call.*

Suddenly, I remembered why I was in Paris after all. I'd been so thrilled by all I'd seen, I'd momentarily forgotten. As I stood reading the message on the card, I also became aware of my wet left foot. I sloshed over to my suitcases and began to unpack. After all, I had important government business to take care of here, as well as taking in the sights. I'd barely finished unpacking and putting my sodden left shoe on a windowsill to dry when the phone rang.

"Allo, Doris Fein ici," I said.

"Demeter," said a voice with a Midwestern US accent.

"Ceres," I replied, giving the countersign.

"Welcome to Paris, Ms. Fein," the voice said. "You will undoubtedly wish to see the sights. We suggest that at twelve noon the day after tomorrow, you should see the Mona Lisa at the Louvre, which is near—"

"I know where the Louvre is; doesn't everyone?" I put in.

"Very well. Be in front of the Mona Lisa at noon. You will be met by a French national five feet six inches in height, male Caucasian, with dark hair and blue eyes. His name is Roger Boucher. He will identify himself to you with the passwords already assigned. You will then give Monsieur Boucher a token of our esteem. Do you understand what is meant?"

"Of course."

"Very well. Enjoy Paris," the voice said. I knew what was coming and said in unison with the voice, "It's the City of Lights." Whoever the voice was, he was not amused. There was a click, and I was staring at a dead phone.

The lobby clock at the Henri IV read three thirty as I left the hotel to see some sights. Knowing that I wasn't due to pick up my spying duties for another day and a half, I felt no conscience pangs about having a good time. As it was getting late in the afternoon, I decided to stay close to the hotel and sightsee on foot.

The Henri IV is just off the Champs Elysées, the most fashionable avenue in Paris. To call the Champs a street or boulevard is an understatement. The main part of the thoroughfare is wide enough to accommodate an army marching. In fact it has, on numerous occasions. If the main part of the Champs wasn't wide enough, there were also two, what would you call them? . . . service roads, I guess, alongside the vehicular part of the roadway.

Lining the inside service roads are shops and seemingly an endless progression of sidewalk cafés, most of them parts of restaurants. All of them are very, very Parisian and as expensive as they are Gallic. As I walked along the Champs, headed toward the Rond Point, with my back to the Arch of Triumph, it seemed to me that I could have been transported back in time to the glories of the French Empire. All except for the occasional place advertising cheese-burgers and hamburgers.

After a while, I began to get pains in my legs and feet from the long walk I'd been taking. I knew it was time to return to the hotel. I know my limits when it comes to being a pedestrian. I'm just not accustomed to walking as a way to get places. The Californian doesn't walk. Anywhere. In fact, when a Californian, who drives everywhere he goes, feels the lack of exercise, he will drive to a place where exercise takes place. Like a spa. But walk? It's somehow déclassé.

Rather than take the same route back to my hotel, I turned off the Champs Elysées and into a side street. Not knowing Paris, I assumed that one can walk around the block and be back at his starting place. Wrong. There seems to be no order nor reason in the way the City of Lights is laid out. I hadn't been strolling on side streets for more than a few minutes when I discovered I was absolutely lost.

But if you're going to be lost someplace, Paris certainly beats any other. Unlike many big cities, it seems that in Paris, people live everywhere. In New York, you'd be hard pressed to find someone walking around the financial district after business hours are done. Wall Street is a desert on Sundays. Here, you can find people living in the heart of a business district.

And where people live, as in a neighborhood, you'll find the shops where they buy their necessities.

In the space of one block, I passed three bakeries. As I gazed in a display window at some incredible pastries, I heard a grunt from Petunia reminding me that I hadn't eaten since my plane landed. I fought it valiantly but, in the end, Petunia won.

I had no trouble in the pastry shop. Like almost everyone I'd met in Paris, the lady behind the counter spoke some English. I bought a scrumptious-looking fruit tart and, heaven help me, two Napoleons. I mean, after all, when one is in Paris, the least one can do is try out anything named Napoleon. Within reason, of course.

I'd intended to wait until I returned to the Henri IV before I opened the paper box containing my pastries. I really had. But as I strolled past the windows of one store after another, my resolve weakened. Then when I saw a blue-overalled workman sitting down at the edge of the fountain of a little, almost-hidden square, eating a half loaf of Parisian bread with cheese, I gave up on my will power completely. I opened the box of pastry and took out the fruit tart.

I looked around me and tried in vain to figure out where I was in reference to my hotel, but couldn't. If I were anywhere near the Arch of Triumph, I could have used that as a guide. But in the little side streets, you can't see anything but the close-set buildings and shops. In a way, walking the side streets of Paris, you could be in the mid-nineteenth century, not the late twentieth. Unless you chose to notice the women wearing unbelievably tight jeans with straight legs and (tacky) spike heels and western shirts. The outfit may be considered chic, but with my shape . . . out of the question.

I was about to try my French on any passerby, asking directions to the Champs Elysées, when through an alleyway I caught a glimpse of the Arch of Triumph. I turned down the alley and promptly ran across an incredible little shop that sold nothing but antique bottles. So help me, that's all. But there were some exquisite examples of the glassmaker's art in that window. I didn't go inside; I stood on the teeny sidewalk and feasted my eyes on the bottles, phials, and perfume flacons while I was finishing off my fruit tart.

I had my eye on a rare venetian bottle that rested on the top shelf of the window display. As I'm rather short by American standards, I backed off a few steps into the street, the better to see the top display row in the window. As I did, I heard a loud honk behind me, and felt a sharp bump smack in the middle of the right part of my southbound anatomy. It didn't hurt, really. It was as though someone had hit me in the rear with a well-placed barefoot kick.

Off balance, I fell forward. The last mouthful of fruit tart, however, didn't stay where it was in my hand. From the jolt, the tart aimed for my mouth ended up midway between my nose and hairline. Did I mention it was a blueberry tart? It definitely clashed with the tan pants suit I was wearing.

I spun around with pastry on my face and indignation in my heart. Then I saw what had hit me in the dignity. It was a Rolls-Royce Corniche convertible, silver gray with the top down. The car was large enough to have negotiated the narrow alley, but just. When I'd taken one step back to admire the bottle shop window, there had been just enough overhang from the previously mentioned ample Fein derrière to be nudged by the Rolls's front right fender.

But as gorgeous as the automobile was, it was nothing compared to the driver! He was dressed in designer jeans, with a sweater over a western shirt. On his feet were western boots that had to be ostrich skin. And on the most incredibly handsome face I'd seen outside of movies, he wore a look of deep concern. He bolted from the driver's seat of the Rolls and to my side.

By the time I regained my balance, he was there, helping me. Up close, he was even more gorgeous than from a distance. He was a shade over six feet tall, with dark hair, clear skin, and the deepest blue eyes. As he took my arm, I caught a scent of a very expensive men's cologne. He looked so much like the French movie star Alain Delon that I stood and gaped at him while he spoke to me in rapid-fire French.

My French is perfectly acceptable in a slow conversation, on topics basic to getting along in a non-English-speaking situation. But when someone really cranks up in French, I get one word in five, at best.

I knew that this handsome apparition was asking me if I was hurt, but not much more. I groped for the proper phrase in French to ease his concern, but all I could come out with was, *"Je suis okay. Tout va bien."*

"But you are *américaine!"* he exclaimed in delightfully accented English. He favored me with a smile my Uncle Saul would have adored for its perfection. He took a pocket handkerchief from his jeans pocket. I haven't seen a pocket handkerchief on a man under fifty in my entire life. In fact the only man I've ever seen who carries one is Harry Grubb, an eighty-year-old friend of mine, back in Santa Amelia, California. This handsome man's handkerchief had the same scent as he was wearing. He began dabbing at my face with the linen. I didn't know why at first, until I caught a glimpse of my clown-like tart makeup coming off on what must have been an expensive noseblow, indeed. It was monogrammed with a single letter "F."

"Are you hurt?" he asked.

"Only my dignity," I replied, with great grasp of euphemism.

"I am so sorry," he said. "But you stepped right in front of my *voiture.* I could not stop in time. I couldn't sound the hooter in time, either," he concluded.

From all my Agatha Christie books, I knew what the handsome chap meant when he said "hooter." In continental English, a hooter is a car horn. In California, it's a funny joke.

"It's all right, really," I said. "It was my own fault. I stepped back to get a better look at that venetian glass bottle there." I indicated the exquisite blue decanter in the shop window.

"An imitation," he said in his charming accent.

"How can you tell that at a glance?" I asked.

"Bottles are my business, in a way," he said. "I am Claude Fitzroi," he finished and stood there smiling.

I knew from the way he said his name that I was supposed to recognize it. But heaven help me, I didn't. I stood there and smiled. He must have seen that I was looking blank in response to his name. He smiled ruefully and, as he dabbed at my face with his handkerchief, he directed my attention to a small bistro alongside the bottle shop. Then the name clicked in my mind. For there, amid the many advertisements for Cinzano, Pernod, and the like was a four-colored enameled sign that read: FITZROI, LE MEILLEUR COGNAC DU MONDE—the best cognac in the world.

I salvaged the situation as best I could by saying, "Oh, *that* Fitzroi."

"*Oui, mademoiselle, that* Fitzroi," he replied. I just *loved* the way he pronounced mademoiselle. Then again, someone can ask the way to the ladies' room in French and, to me, it sounds *charmant.*

"My family has been putting fine cognac into bottles of all sorts for hundreds of years," Fitzroi explained. "I am, myself, a connoisseur of antique bottles. That is how I know this bottle you desire is an imitation, *mademoiselle* . . . I am sorry. You have the advantage of me."

"Fein," I said. "Doris Fein." I gave the "Doris" the French pronunciation: *Doh-ree*. I think it sounds nicer.

"*Enchanté,*" Fitzroi said, extending his hand. I took it, and he gave me that European handshake men give to women on the Continent: one downward shake and a quick release. It's really too bad about the quick release part, too. I could have spent some time just holding hands.

All this time, I'm afraid I was looking at Claude Fitzroi the same way Petunia would regard a banana split with all the trimmings. It's hard to explain this to any woman who never had braces on her teeth or shopped in half sizes. But when a blindingly handsome, obviously rich Frenchman holds your hand, it's hard to let go. You're afraid you'll wake up at any moment!

The spell was rudely broken by a hoot of a Paris taxicab horn and a spate of obscenities from its driver. A taxicab had come down the narrow alley and was unable to pass until Claude Fitzroi moved his Rolls Corniche. From what I could understand of the cabdriver's tirade, it had to do with the arrogance of filthy rich dirty-thus-and-suches who keep a hard-working cabdriver from making a decent living.

"We must go, Doh-ree," Fitzroi said. "We are halting progress, it seems. May I drive you someplace?"

"I've been warned about getting into cars with strange men," I said, half seriously.

"Ah, but we are no longer strangers, are we?" said Fitzroi smoothly, as he led me to the passenger side of his Rolls. I protested no further. I've never ridden in any model of a Rolls-Royce, let alone a convertible. "And with the hood down," Fitzroi continued, "we are in plain view, you and I. Surely, you are safe?"

"Surely," I said.

Funny, though. Maybe it's because of my Californian upbringing, but I didn't worry about being safe with this comparative stranger. He was driving a Rolls. I hate to admit it but, to a large extent, the people in California tend to judge each other by what sort of car they drive. Not unlike people in other cities judge people by what they wear. And face it. There's something so terribly *respectable* about someone who drives a car worth over a hundred thousand dollars!

"Where are you stopping?" Fitzroi asked as we pulled away in eerie silence.

"The Henri IV," I said.

"Excellent!" he replied. "One of our more comfortable hotels. Of course, you will not eat in their restaurant."

"That bad?" I asked.

"On the contrary," he said. "It's an outstanding restaurant. I meant simply that there are other places. One of them is where I shall take you for dinner this evening."

"I never said anything about dinner," I said.

"An oversight on your part, I am sure," said Fitzroi easily. "But for your welfare, I must insist that I accompany you for the balance of the day and night."

"For my welfare?" I asked. "What has this to do with my well-being?"

Claude Fitzroi made a turn onto the Champs Elysées. It had been only a few yards from the alley where we'd met. "Well, you have been struck by a motorcar," Claude said. "You feel fine now, but who knows? You could collapse later. You might have a concussion, you know."

"If you'll forgive a slightly vulgar reference," I replied, "people seldom get concussions when they're hit in the place your car hit me."

We both laughed and, by the time he dropped me at the Henri IV, it was "Claude" and "Dohree" and we had a date for dinner. I really didn't have to take the elevator to my room. I could have floated.

4

When Claude Fitzroi telephoned my room from the lobby at seven o'clock promptly, I still wasn't dressed. Since he'd dropped me off at the Henri IV, I had tried on every item in my new wardrobe at least once. I'd narrowed the choice down to a smart new suit in blue or an out-and-out dressy dress in black. I was standing in the middle of my bedroom in panty hose when the phone rang.

"*Allo,* Dohree. This is Claude."

"Oh, gee," I said, "this is terrible!"

"Something is wrong?" Claude asked, concern showing in his voice.

"No, no," I hedged. "But I'm still not dressed. You didn't say where we were having dinner. I didn't know what to wear. What are you wearing?" I figured if Claude was wearing a suit, I'd wear the dress. If he wasn't, then back-to-the-old-Gucci-suitcase.

"I am wearing a simple, dark cocktail dress," he said facetiously, "with no jewelry, shoes suitable for disco dancing, and a light evening wrap."

Now, that's *savoir faire.* To spare me any embarrassment, Claude suggested what I should wear, all the time making it a joke at his expense. Ah, the

71

French! "I'll be down in fifteen minutes," I said. I made it in ten.

I've never been impressed by wealth, nor have I ever been enchanted with money, per se. I can count among my true friends one genuine millionaire, Harry Grubb. But there is no denying that most of the world *is* impressed by money and acts accordingly. When Claude and I pulled up at the Grand Moulin restaurant, you would have thought that royalty had arrived in a Rolls. Even in New York City, where I have dined at the finest places, I never saw service like this! I suppose if one is very wealthy in Europe, he must spend a good deal of money on Chap-Stik alone. Various parts of a rich person's anatomy must get chapped from others' kissing. Both figuratively and literally.

The Grand Moulin was decorated in the French equivalent of the Gay Nineties. In France, they called it *la belle époque.* There were Lautrec posters in the foyer, and I realized with a sharp intake of breath that they weren't reproductions. Nor were some paintings inside the main dining room copies, either. I saw several great names of the French Impressionist school casually hanging in small alcoves in the dining room.

A *maître d'hôtel,* who was dressed in white tie and could have stepped out of a movie, led us across the room. He walked directly toward one of those small alcoves I mentioned. To my surprise, he pushed on the side of the wall, and a door opened onto a corridor leading to a small flight of stairs. I looked askance at Claude.

"This is a very old, very famous restaurant," Claude explained. "It was opened during the 1880s. This passage leads to their private dining rooms. It is said that King Edward VII used to dine here with Lily Langtry. Of course, Edward was then the Prince of Wales."

This was something I knew about. In Victorian days, the more notoriously libidinous noblemen would meet their mistresses in the discreet privacy of small dining rooms like those offered by the Grand Moulin. It was also said that some very naughty doings took place in these rooms. All to the tune of blindfolded violinists and the popping of champagne corks.

The *maître d'* led us to a door and opened it to disclose a room that could have been used for such intimate dinners nearly a century ago. The room was wainscoted in dark wood paneling and red-flocked wallpaper. Real illuminating-gas fixtures flickered in sconces on the walls. And the table!

The centerpiece was a fully feathered pheasant. I discovered later that the pheasant had already been cooked, boned, then remounted on the rack, with the feathers added for color. Candlesticks that had to be solid silver cast a cheery light onto the spotless white napery and gleaming knives and forks. There were spoons and odd-shaped utensils for eating I'd never seen before. A magnum of champagne rested alongside the table in a silver cooler. In addition to the table and chairs, I quickly noted an overstuffed chaise longue and a larger couch in one corner of the room.

I made a mental note to inform Monsieur Fitzroi, once we were alone, not to expect he was dining with a pushover just because the room had a history of assignations.

Claude spoke in rapid French with the *maître d'hôtel*. I could tell that he was specifying wines and certain extras. Petunia grunted approval. I was being nonchalant while this went on, feigning interest in the artwork that hung in heavy gilt frames on the walls. Then I suddenly realized what I was looking at in those frames!

At first glance, the pictures were of seemingly high-born ladies and gentlemen having dinner in just such a room as this. But as I moved from one print to another, I saw they were in sequence. By the time the sequence ended, the ladies and gentlemen were definitely not dressed . . . for dinner, anyway. Face flaming, I quickly took the chair that the *maitre d'* pulled back from the table for me.

The *maitre d'* left the room, and I sat opposite Claude, wondering what to say. Or do. What did he expect? What I didn't expect him to do was to burst out laughing.

"Oh, Dohree," he laughed. "The expression on your face!"

"I was admiring the artwork. Until I realized what

it was," I said stiffly. "And it made me wonder what you thought *I* was."

"Ah, but I know what you are." Fitzroi smiled. "You are a charming, lovely young woman. You laugh at the right things; you are easy to be with. You are a tourist come to enjoy Paris."

"Right on, *monsieur*," I said. "The city; not the citizens."

Claude shrugged his shoulders and spread his hands apart. "But that is all I have offered, Dohree," he said. "It is true that this place has a rather . . . um, naughty reputation. But that is only in history books. For the most part, the people who dine in these private rooms aren't lovers. They are businessmen, conducting high-level deals requiring privacy. I'm afraid you will find there has been more of a financial history to these rooms than one of . . . what do you say? Fooling around?"

"I just didn't want to give the impression that I . . ."

"Was here for some hanky-panky?" Claude finished.

I burst out laughing. First off, Claude using such an old-fashioned term was funny. Then when he pronounced the phrase with his accent, it came out "ahnkee-pahnkee." Abruptly, all tension went out of the situation.

Just then, there was a knock at the door. It was our waiter, bringing the first of what seemed like endless courses of a dinner fit for an emperor. The scents and sights of that incomparable meal soon caused a series of snuffles and grunts from Petunia. Both Petunia and I fell to with great *élan,* as the French say.

By the time we had finished dinner and Claude was lingering over a huge balloon glass of guess whose brand of cognac, I'd learned a great deal about Claude.

He's thirty-two years old, and the sole heir to the entire cognac firm that bears his family name. He was educated in France, England, and the United States. He spent a year or two in New York City, doing graduate work at Columbia University.

I didn't inquire, but Claude volunteered the fact that he is unmarried. He loves music of all kinds, except the opera. It seems that when he was a small boy, his parents used to drag him to their season box at the Paris opera, and he always hated it. He and I found common ground in our mutual liking of most rock music, though.

"But one cannot find really good rock music in Paris," Claude said. "For that, one must go either to England or the USA." His face brightened then. "But I do know a place where one may hear an American rock group. And one may dance. Would you care to go?"

Truth to tell, I felt stuffed to the gills on dinner. The very thought of dancing was taxing. And I was beginning to feel the effects of jet lag. Claude was still awaiting my answer about dancing.

"I don't know, Claude," I said. "It's been a long

day. And it was a very heavy dinner. . . ."

"Fresh air!" said Claude, snapping his fingers.
"That is all you really need. To blow away the cob-
webs of the mind. Would you care to walk through
some Paris streets with me?"

"But what about your car?" I asked.

"A mere nothing," Claude replied with an airy
wave of his hand. "I will leave it here, at the Grand
Moulin."

"Will it be all right?" I asked. I was thinking about
that expensive car unwatched.

"But of course, Dohree." He laughed. "Who would
steal a Rolls? Where could you hide such a thing, or
sell it? It's like stealing someone's elephant. You may
get away with it initially but, after a time, people will
notice what you are keeping in your backyard."

I had to admit the logic of what Claude said. He
called for the check and, when the waiter returned,
I gave him a gaze of wintry calm in response to the
almost-leer he had on his face. I guess he expected to
see me somewhat disheveled after an *intime* dinner
in a private dining room.

We walked down the street outside the Grand
Moulin, after being bowed out of the establishment
by what seemed like the whole restaurant staff. The
Grand Moulin is on the Right Bank of the river Seine,
which bisects Paris. But we were close to the Tuileries gardens and strolled that way, over the grounds.

It's a lovely park, with statuary and little walks. If
one continues walking through the gardens, the

streets lead to a bridge across the river. It's called the Pont du Carrousel. It leads to the quais de Pont Neuf, near where poets and painters have lived since the turn of the century.

Before we left the gardens though, Claude took me by the hand and instructed me to close my eyes. He led me a few steps and told me to open my eyes again. I found myself facing a smaller replica of the Arch of Triumph at the Place du Carrousel. "Now, turn around, Dohree," he said. I did, and caught my breath with a gasp.

For when I turned, I found that I could see directly through the Tuileries gardens, past all the park and directly down the Champs Elysées. At the end of the brilliantly illuminated avenue stood the full-sized Arch of Triumph. All along the way, streetlights on the Champs were blazing. The thrill of that sight, surrounded by the Tuileries in the moonlight, was not to be believed! As I stood there, Claude took my face in both his hands and planted a thoroughly Gallic kiss on my lips.

"You are a lovely young woman, Dohree," he said gently in my ear as he nuzzled at my neck.

"You're pretty swift, yourself," I replied amid goosebumps. After that, I had no trouble staying awake. We walked across the Pont du Carrousel to the other side. There, Claude hailed a taxi.

The disco we went to was not unlike any disco anywhere else. It was *loud*, crowded, and people were waiting in line to get in. But not my charming

Claude. I couldn't tell if money changed hands between him and the doorman, but again we were bowed and scraped at when we entered the place. I don't know how long we danced, or how many glasses of champagne we drank. But I'm what you call a nip and tuck drinker. One nip and you can tuck me away for the night. However, if one stays active, as I was doing, I suppose the body throws off the effects of bubbly wine. When we finally left the disco, we walked a few blocks, then Claude got another cab. I'd mention what went on in the cab on the way back to my hotel, but I'm sure you can fill in the blanks.

Claude saw me to the door of my suite. I was hesitating as to whether I should ask him in or not. I guess I should explain. I know the rules of the man-woman game; I'm not naive. But knowing the rules doesn't mean I've been a participant. I'm a virgin. It may seem quaint in this day and age, but there you are. Or here I am. The combination of Paris, this exquisitely handsome man, an evening of champagne and dancing, all combined to melt my reserve. I was about to open the door to my suite and ask him in. While I was thinking of a way to phrase my invitation, Claude surprised me by taking me in his arms and kissing me in a fashion that was more friendly than French.

"I am desolate, Dohree," he said. "But I must go." And before I could say another word, he was striding down the corridor to the elevators. He turned at the elevator gate and gave me a dazzling smile. "I will call you tomorrow," he said. *"A demain!"* The lift came and my prince charming disappeared.

I am not given to vulgarity or profanity. My upbringing, I guess. But as I saw Claude go, I said aloud, "Well, I'll be damned!" All night long, he'd been breathing heavily in my ear. The cab ride home was simply *torrid.* Then, a peck and good-bye! As I opened the door to my suite and switched on the lights, I was crushed. Had my deodorant failed or something? Then when I saw my suite, I let out a yelp!

Everything was upside down. The contents of my suitcases were strewn from one end of the suite to the other. My closets had been emptied out and from what I could see, the clothing slashed! My new Gucci luggage had received similar treatment, and it rested in tatters among the other mutilated items.

It took me a moment or two for it all to register. My parcel! Someone or ones had searched my room for the parcel I was concealing in the flush tank of the bathroom! I dashed into my bedroom, looking neither right nor left, and ran directly to the old-fashioned john. Before I could clamber up onto the seat and check for my package, I heard a man's voice say from my bedroom.

"Don't bother, Ms. Fein. It's gone. I checked."

I turned and stepped back into my bedroom. Seated on *my* bed was a man I'd never seen before in my life! "Congratulations, Ms. Fein," the man said.

"You have managed to completely screw up a routine courier assignment. And in the process, you may have precipitated an international crisis. You've had a busy day. I hope you enjoyed yourself!"

5

I'd estimate that the man was in his mid-fifties. He was dressed in the same three-piece blue pinstripe suit one sees on bankers and brokers. He was perched on the edge of my bed, posing like one of those fairy-tale illustrations of an elf on a mushroom. He had one knee up and was clasping it with both hands.

Perhaps the elfin resemblance was enhanced by his size. He was a very short man, with delicate hands and features. His full head of hair was snow white, his eyebrows and mustache darker and shot with gray. His eyebrows were tufted, giving him even more of a puckish look. He did not seem amused.

"Who are you? And how do you know who I am?" I began.

"Please, Ms. Fein," he said, holding up a hand like a toy traffic cop. "First off . . . Demeter," he said, giving the password. "That should convince you I'm not a burglar." He paused and arched his pointy eyebrows at me until I gave the countersign, Ceres.

"Now, wasn't that economical?" said the elfin man in a surprisingly deep voice. "I have saved us all those silly questions you were about to ask. And naturally, you'll want to see this, too."

He reached inside his coat pocket and produced a US diplomatic passport, which he casually flipped at me. I caught it on the wing and examined the thing. It identified my small caller as Cody Garrett, age fifty-six, born in Michigan. He had the one passport picture I've encountered that truly looked like its subject. On the passport picture, Garrett was smiling. Seated on my bed, he wasn't. In fact, he wore an expression that subtly blended concern, annoyance, and utter condescension toward me. I can't say what my face looked like when he said, "You've botched it completely, Ms. Fein. I am here to pick up the pieces."

"I've botched what?" I said, playing it cagey. The fact that this man knew the password and countersign didn't mean he was worthy of confidence. I'd used those passwords over the phone, earlier in the day. They could have been overheard.

"Oh, my dear Ms. Fein," he said wearily, "it's late. I was rather hoping we could do without all this. But here goes. I am Cody Garrett. I am the second economic attaché to the US Embassy, here in Paris. That's my job for publication. On the quiet side, I am the bureau chief of the Organization in France. It was I who spoke to you today and gave you instructions."

Suddenly, it clicked. Garrett's voice had seemed familiar, with its Midwest accent. But the deep voice that came out of such a diminutive man had momentarily confused me. His voice just didn't match his appearance. "I recognize your voice now," I said.

"Good, good," said Garrett. "Now as to the assignment you've bungled so badly—let's see what can be done."

"You're quite certain that the parcel I was carrying is gone?" I asked, hoping against hope.

"Positive," said Garrett. "I checked it out."

"But how?" I said, remembering the wet-foot incident earlier. "You're shorter than I am. I could barely get the package into the flush tank."

Garrett reached behind him on my bed and produced a hand mirror. "Simple," he said. "All one has to do is take a chair, like that one"—he indicated one of my bedroom chairs—"and stand on it alongside the fixture in the bath. Holding this mirror above one's head, the entire contents of the flush tank are visible. I assure you, Ms. Fein, the parcel is not there."

"Oh."

"Oh, indeed, Ms. Fein," he mocked. "And now that we're both satisfied the parcel is gone, we should try to determine who has stolen it."

"Who? Don't you mean what government?" I asked. "What would an individual do with that enzyme sample?"

"My turn," said Garrett. "What enzyme sample?"

"The plant-growth enzyme," I said. "The one for growing crops all year round."

The little man burst into laughter. "Plant enzyme!" he chortled. "Oh my, my, my! Really, Ms.

Fein, you are delightfully naive. I didn't think the Organization still used that fairy tale!"

"Just a minute," I said. "I'm beginning to smell a rat. And his initials are George Case."

The little man dropped his look of amusement-at-my-expense. He stood up and straightened to his full height. He was so erect and so dignified, he looked like nothing more than a toy soldier in mufti. He crossed over to me and extended his hand.

"I can see that you are no one's career agent, Ms. Fein," he said. "Perhaps my humor has grown somewhat insular, if not institutional. We've got off on the wrong foot. Shall we begin again at shaking hands?"

Still not having the remotest idea of what the man was talking about, I shook his hand. I mean, even if he had been truly nasty to me earlier, this was an unmistakable overture to friendship. "Now that we're no longer at war with each other," I said, "is it too much to ask what in the world is going on?"

"Not at all," Garrett said. "But I noticed an unopened wine bottle in the other room. I've been here without dinner, waiting for your return. Do you mind awfully if we continue this in what's left of your sitting room? I've heard much of bedroom diplomacy, but this isn't my idea of it."

When we went back into the sitting room, I became aware of just how much damage had been done to the room as well as my wardrobe and luggage. It broke my heart to see my clothes the way they were. But I could only imagine how the hotel management was going to feel!

Garrett righted one of the lovely gilt chairs in the sitting room and, ignoring its slashed seat cushion, sat down. He reached over casually to the wine cooler, which was the only piece of furniture in the room that appeared undisturbed. With a motion that bespoke years of practice, he lifted the bottle of Dom Perignon from the cooler. Though the ice had long since melted, Garrett didn't get so much as a drop of water on his blue pinstripe suit. He arched his pointy brows at the date on the label and, satisfied, carefully opened the Dom Perignon. He opened the bottle with only a moist plop as the cork came out. I know that's the proper way to do it, though most people prefer to hear the cork pop.

Garrett accomplished the maneuver with such fluid ease that I no longer doubted his cover as a career diplomat. The wine glasses were unbroken on the stand, and we shared a mocking toast to the chaos about us. I sat down on a badly slashed sofa and listened as the elegant elf spoke.

"Ms. Fein, in every line of work there are practical jokes that are played on newcomers and apprentices. In the main, they are crude, but some bizarre tradition insists they are perpetuated. The apprentice painter is sent off to fetch a bucket of polka dot paint. The new recruit in the army is dispatched to get the canon report."

"Or the old bucket of steam play," I offered.

"Exactly," said Garrett, smiling warmly. "And

the IGO is no exception," he added with a rueful smile. "It's been tradition in the Organization that when a fledgling courier inquires as to what he's carrying—"

"Or *she* is carrying," I put in.

"Forgive me, Ms. Fein," Garrett said. "I'm of the old guard, you know. I've remembered your honorific as *Ms.* But please. It's too late in my life for relearning my pronouns. May I proceed without fear of being labeled sexist?"

"Please do," I said.

"In any event, the very point of being a courier is to have no curiosity about what you carry. But it seems everyone—on *his* or *her* first mission—wants to know. It's only human. I have to admit that I did too."

"Welcome to the ranks of humanity, Mr. Garrett," I sniped.

"I shan't dignify that last," Garrett said. "I'll tell you that the plant-growth enzyme is a fiction. Just like a left-handed monkey wrench. Case told you that tale to satisfy your curiosity, no more."

"Of all the high-handed condescending—"

"Yes, all of those things, Ms. Fein. But it was none of your business what you carried. I mocked you for unprofessional behavior. I didn't realize that you were an utter amateur that Case was using as a mule."

"A *what?*" I exclaimed, feeling my anger rise.

"No, no. I can see you misunderstand," Garrett

said. "A mule is a smuggler's term. It means someone who has never smuggled anything in his life, and is doing it just once. In that way, there is little suspicion of the mule. Often, the mule performs the duty never knowing what has been smuggled."

"In other words, I'm a dupe."

"*You* said that, Ms. Fein. I find *mule* kinder."

"And you are a diplomat, Mr. Garrett."

"I like to think so," he said. "It's my life's work."

"Then can you tell me in plain talk what in the name of heaven has been going on?" I asked. I expected some evasion and uneasy shifting of eyes, as I had seen when George Case lied to me.

But Garrett said to me in utter sincerity, "Why not? You've been ill-used in this affair, Ms. Fein. I have a granddaughter not quite your age. I wouldn't have put her in a situation like this. I find George Case doing it unconscionable. I feel you're entitled to an explanation."

Garrett refilled his champagne glass and offered to refill mine. I surprised myself when I accepted. But there was something about this half-size dandy that somehow engendered respect and obedience. Garrett took a sip of champagne and began.

"What you were carrying was a statuette. A figurine, actually. It was an image of a boyar, a tsarist Russian aristocrat. It was just five inches high, including its filigree gold base, set with seed pearls and diamonds. The manikin itself is enameled and similarly gem encrusted. It is carved from a single crystal of rose quartz."

"It sounds beautiful," I said, secretly regretting now that I hadn't peeked when I had the chance.

"Oh, it is," Garrett said. "Beautiful until you realize its incredibly bloody past. Then it's not quite so lovely a piece. It was one of a set of twenty-four historical Russian soldiers. It was commissioned by the last tsar of Russia, Nicholas the Second. The figures were each as perfect an example of Carl Fabergé's work as ever seen." Garrett arched his eyebrows. "You *do* know of Fabergé, don't you?"

"Yes, I do. I saw an exhibit of Fabergé work at the art museum in Los Angeles last year." I began to appreciate what Garrett was saying. Fabergé was an incredible designer of—well, *things.* He would take an item like a matchbox for the tsar and render it in hammered gold. Or a desk set made of sculpted jade. You couldn't exactly call Fabergé a silversmith, or a jeweler either. I guess the words are master artisan. I also know that Fabergé's work is priceless.

"Then imagine, if you will," Garrett said, "an entire set of twenty-four figures, each more exquisite than the next. And then, once envisioned, realize that they were merely a set of toy soldiers. A birthday present for the young tsarevitch, Alexis."

"Some birthday present for a kid," I said.

"Not when you realize the opulence of tsarist Russia," Garrett said. "The little Alexis was a delicate child. He suffered from hemophilia. All his toys were elaborate. He spent so much time in bed, recovering from even slight injuries. Young Alexis had a collection of toys that were partly playthings and partly works of art. Superb works of art, in this case."

"And I was carrying one of those toy soldiers."

"A very crucial one, Ms. Fein," Garrett said. "The collection was in the tsarevitch Alexis' possession when he and his family were murdered at Ekaterinburg in 1918. Like many of the tsarist treasures, the collection never did find its way to the People's Museum. It vanished. Undoubtedly, the men who killed the royal family looted their effects afterwards."

I felt a small shiver run up my back. I had read the book *Nicholas and Alexandra* as a history assignment in school. The Romanovs may have been bad rulers, but to kill them the way the Bolsheviks had! Alexis, the prince, had been only thirteen. And sick. He would have most likely died young anyway. But to picture their murderers picking through their personal effects. It was all so grisly!

I told Garrett how I felt. He replied, "Oddly enough, it was a break for the world of art. The men who slew the royal family knew the value of the figures. An ignorant peasant would have broken up the figurines for the gems. We know that the set was intact as recently as 1939, just before World War II."

"How did you find out about that?" I asked. "I know that the IGO was formed after World War II ended."

Garrett raised his eyebrows. "Perhaps Case was right in recruiting you, Ms. Fein. You have a good mind. You ask proper questions."

"Thank you," I said. It seemed uncivil to point out that he hadn't answered my question.

"Not at all. Anyway, we knew of the collection being intact in 1939 because one of our people saw it. It was in Istanbul. A diplomat there was approached as a potential customer. Pity he didn't buy it."

"How come?"

"Even in 1939, the asking price was a quarter of a million dollars. In today's currency, that translates into many times the original figure. And bear in mind, the price asked was only a fraction of its real value. The seller had fled Russia and was desperately in need of money. The sale was never consummated and the seller was found floating in the Bosporus with his throat cut."

"And the collection?" I asked.

"Nothing heard of it until after World War II," Garrett said. "It was rumored that King Farouk of Egypt had the figurines. When Farouk was booted out of Egypt, we heard rumors again that the entire collection was for sale. This time, there was no lack of buyers. The only trouble was, the agent in charge of selling the figurines disappeared. A man answering his description was found shot to death in the streets of Buenos Aires in the early 1960s. Are you counting, Ms. Fein? That adds up to ten dead, counting the tsar's family."

"You're right; the things do have a bloody past."

"Ah, but I'm not done yet. The collection had passed into the hands of the Argentinian dictator, Juan Perón. It was said he gave the figures to his wife Eva one Christmas. Whoever acquired the set after the Perón regime fell evidently was seeing hard times. Some of the figurines began to appear in private collections. We know this from word of mouth. No one could possibly acknowledge ownership of the collection. The Russian government has a claim on it, you see."

"Is it a valid claim?" I asked.

"What comprises a valid claim?" Garrett said, sipping at his drink. "You could argue the collection belongs to them. You could also argue it belongs to whoever has it in his possession."

"Then who has it now?"

"We do, Ms. Fein. The United States government has it. Well, not quite. We have all but two of the figurines. A few days ago, we had all but one of them."

The unspoken implication that I had lost one of the figures hung heavy in the air. I tried to gloss over the sad state of affairs. "But how did the government get them? And why?" I asked.

"We acquired the collection almost piecemeal. The largest single acquisition was a dozen of the figures," Garrett said. "As to why, well, Ms. Fein, we have a customer for them."

"But who could buy them all?" I queried. "The whole set must be worth . . ."

"About six million dollars," Garrett finished. "Individually, they might add up to, say . . . four million —five. But owning the entire collection, the price goes up to the higher figure."

"Who in the world could buy it, then?"

An angry look passed over Garrett's face. "There is a prince in an oil-rich country who wants them. He has told our government that unless he gets the collection, the price of crude oil per barrel to the USA will increase by sixty percent. As he is also the spiritual leader of several millions of souls in the Middle East, any increase in oil prices he makes will be followed by the rest of the OPEC nations. Unless, of course, we get him his play toys."

"That's little more than blackmail!" I exclaimed. "You mean that this man is holding up the entire Western bloc of nations for some . . ."

"Toy soldiers," Garrett said bitterly. "And there isn't a thing we can do about it. We can't even say aloud that we have almost all the set. That would cause another crisis with the Soviet Union. We can afford that as easily as another price increase in crude oil."

"And I had one of the last two figures stolen from me," I said glumly.

"In a very amateurish fashion, I might add," said Garrett. "I don't think the plan would have worked with a trained agent."

"What plan?"

"It's an old ploy," Garrett said. "The opposition

found out somehow what you were carrying. There was a leak somewhere. They then sent a pretty boy to romance you around town while they went through your room here. And found what they wanted. You were so caught up with your lover boy, you wouldn't have noticed."

I let the remark about Claude Fitzroi slide. But I couldn't let Garrett think I was *that* naive. "It had to be a coincidence," I said. "Whoever the thieves were, they waited until I was out."

"They made sure you were out," Garrett said. "They sicced that continental type on you. And you swallowed the bait perfectly. My agents followed you with lover boy when you drove off in the car. But when you slipped out of the Grand Moulin, leaving the car, we lost you for some time. We still don't know who lover boy is."

"For your information," I said indignantly, "he is Claude Fitzroi, heir to the cognac fortune. I told you it was a coincidence!"

"For *your* information, Ms. Fein," Garrett said, "Claude Fitzroi is exactly my age, a bit overweight, and bald. We had dinner together at a diplomatic function last week."

"Then it must have been his son I met," I replied. But inside, I was ready for Garrett's rejoinder.

"Fitzroi is unmarried," said the little man. "In point of fact, he is an acknowledged homosexual. No, Ms. Fein. You have been taken in by one of the oldest ploys in espionage."

I know this will sound silly. I felt silly the moment I said it. It was *so* Californian of me. "But he had a Rolls-Royce!" I wailed.

Garrett examined his fingernails before he let me have it. "Pity it wasn't his," said the elfin man. "You can rent a Rolls in Paris as easily as in Beverly Hills, Ms. Fein. We are tracing that car now. But I don't hold out much hope. I suggest you get yourself together. We must go now."

"But where? Why?"

Garrett arched his eyebrows at me. "Why, to an untappable phone, Ms. Fein. You are going to have to explain to George Case exactly how you were seduced out of the quartz boyar."

As I followed Garrett from my suite, I couldn't help but think, "Some seduction!" I lost what I'd been trusted with. And all I had to show for it was a brotherly kiss from "Fitzroi." I didn't even . . . well, I didn't *even!*

Rome

6

We ended up at a rather nice house in Saint-Cloud, a suburb of Paris. From the outside, it looked like any other well-to-do Parisian's residence. But inside! It was filled with offices and in one of them, I told my tale to George Case on their transatlantic line. I didn't try to make myself look better in Case's eyes. I told the truth as I knew it.

I didn't even protest to Case that he'd lied to me about what was in the parcel. Garrett advised me not to. After all, there had been no reason for me to know. After I'd finished my recitation of ineptitude, there was a long silence at the end of the line. Finally, Case's voice came over the miles of ocean.

"What's done is done," Case said flatly. "You don't have to blame yourself, Doris. Stand by and let me speak with Garrett." I wordlessly handed the phone to Garrett, who took it and said into the receiver, "Garrett here."

He listened for a good while, then he began answering in monosyllables. I sensed he was speaking that way because I was near enough to hear. I pantomimed leaving the room and looked askance at him. He smiled and nodded, waving me out of the room.

I must have sat outside the office for three-quarters of an hour while Garrett spoke with Case. Finally, he emerged from the office, looking grim. He led me to his car and on the way back to Paris, he filled me in on Case's reaction to the recent events. Garrett told me that initially Case had been furious. But once the facts were digested, a new and alternate action had been devised.

"Is there anything I can do to help?" I asked. I still felt guilty about losing the statuette.

"I think you've done quite enough, Ms. Fein," Garrett said. "For the balance of this operation, I intend using only experienced personnel."

"I feel dreadful about this," I explained. "And I'd truly like to help out some way. Isn't there any area, one that doesn't take expertise?"

"Don't tempt me, Ms. Fein," Garrett grumbled. "I must locate another courier within the next twenty-four hours."

"But the boyar is gone. Stolen," I protested.

"Do you recall," Garrett said, "I told you that the IGO had all but one of the figures?"

"Yes. But now, the number has changed. And it's my fault. That's why I want to help."

"Admirable sentiments, but your track record doesn't support trusting you with anything more valuable than paper clips at this point."

"That was unnecessary," I said. "I feel bad enough."

"As well you should," Garrett snapped, showing no

mercy. "But all that is to one side. There is another figurine that must be picked up by courier, in Rome. We still won't have the full set, but lacking just one, we can deliver what we do have to the little brown prince in London. We'll say we have the missing figure and stall him while we try to find the boyar."

"London? What's he doing there?" I queried. "I thought you said he was a Middle East prince."

"He is, he is," said Garrett. "But London has become the playground of oil-rich Arabs of late. There are all the shops, the night life, and above all the casinos. They're private gambling clubs. At least one of them owes its existence to an Arab gambler. He dropped a cool million pounds one night. Never turned a hair, either. But he single-handedly saved the club, which had been in financial straits. You see, the English don't have that kind of money to toss about. Especially not the upper classes."

"You know, I read about that in the papers," I said. "About the Arab who lost a million pounds at the tables. The article said he was back the next night, gambling again."

"Then you know our customer from the Middle East." Garrett smiled. "That's exactly who wants the Fabergé figures. We have all of them in London, save the boyar and a figure of a cossack. The cossack must be picked up in Rome and brought to London."

"Then why don't you have someone who's already in Rome pick it up?"

"Because this operation is run on a need-to-know

basis. The Rome bureau knows nothing about it. To request one of their couriers requires my briefing the Rome bureau chief. And I don't have permission for that. Clearance would take days, and we have only hours. No, Ms. Fein. It must be one of my people. And I am dreadfully shorthanded. Congress has cut our budget to the bone lately."

"Then I'll do it. Go to Rome for you."

"Out of the question. George Case would have kittens when he found out."

"Does he have to know?"

Garrett laughed loud and long. "My dear Doris," he said, "I must report weekly to IGO headquarters on how many hairs I have on my head. This outfit is one of the most completely documented organizations in the world. And while it's true that I'm absolute head of the Paris bureau, there are limits to my authority."

I decided not to pursue the matter any further. We rode in silence for a time. Then suddenly, I thought of the condition of my room and wardrobe back at the hotel. How would I explain all that at the front desk? I mentioned it to Garrett.

"You're lucky I'm not George Case," he said. "He would have left you to explain it yourself. He was quite angry. But don't worry; I'll get you off the hook. You needn't even return there if you have your passport with you."

"I do have it," I said. "But what about my personal things? The wardrobe is shot, but I do have to brush my teeth, comb my hair, and use certain personal items."

"No problem. After I check you into another hotel, I'll talk to the Henri IV management. I'll tell them that your room was burglarized last night, and when you found it ransacked, you called me at the embassy. You were terrified to stay at the Henri IV any longer. I'll say that I've come just to pick up your personal things and to report the incident to the Paris police."

"But won't I have to speak with the police, too?"

"The police will never hear about it, Ms. Fein," said Garrett easily. "The hotel doesn't want any publicity of this sort. Some of the richest people in Europe stay there. The rich must feel safe and secure where they stay. No, I'm sure that if I say you are willing to forget the damage to your property, so will the hotel."

"But the furniture in that room," I protested. "I'm sure it cost much more than anything I lost."

"A lot cheaper for them to redo the room than what they'd lose in guests if the word got out. Oh, it will all work out. Trust me, Ms. Fein."

Within the hour, Garrett had me checked into Le Crebillon, down at the other end of the Champs Elysées from the Henri IV. The elfin man smoothed the way at the check-in and there was no hassle about my lack of luggage.

Le Crebillon is every bit as elegant as the Henri IV, and is decorated in the same nineteenth-century style. I could have spent a fair time just looking at the objets d'art, but all I really wanted at that point was a hot tub and a night's sleep. Once he was sure I was settled in, Garrett took his leave. "Good night, Mr. Garrett," I said.

"*Good-bye,* Ms. Fein," he said pointedly. "A messenger will bring over whatever is salvageable tomor—" He glanced at his watch and shook his head. "This morning," he corrected. He gave me a little nod, then left.

As I didn't have a toothbrush, I did my best with a washcloth, took a brief tub, and was soon in the large soft bed. I didn't so much as dream. The next thing I knew, it was morning, and the telephone was ringing. The messenger was downstairs with my effects. The hotel would send the package up with a bellman, and did I want breakfast in my room? I sure did.

As I looked over my things, I could have cried. The only undamaged items in my entire wardrobe were three pairs of shoes, my toothbrush, and some personal items; even my makeup case was slashed. There was one other thing in the plastic sack my effects had arrived in. It was a typewritten note that said: *Must see you immediately. Call me at 865 66 20. Garrett.*

I cleaned up as best I could and donned the cocktail dress I had worn all through the night's activities. Then I settled down to the modest breakfast I'd ordered at Petunia's urging: a heavenly mushroom omclette, *croissants,* and *café au lait.* Once Petunia had quieted down, I called the number on the note. It must have been Garrett's private line, for it was he, not a secretary, who answered. "Garrett here."

"This is Doris Fein," I began.

"Not on the telephone," said Garrett quickly. "I'll pick you up there. Be in the lobby that faces the rue Cambon in . . . one hour. Be sure you have the right lobby. There are two, you know."

"I'm sorry," I came back. "You'll have to pick me up in my room. I refuse to be seen in the lobby of Le Crebillon wearing last night's dress."

"Very well," Garrett said impatiently. "But I can assure you that any Parisian who saw you couldn't care less. And even if they did, they wouldn't mention it."

"It's what *I* think that matters," I explained. "So, if you can find me some sort of trench coat, I'd appreciate it."

"In one hour," said Garrett, hanging up.

Garrett arrived precisely on time, carrying a woman's raincoat. "One of our cipher clerks is about your size," Garrett explained. "But you must arrange to have this coat sent back, once you're done with it."

"What's up?" I asked without amenities. "I thought last night that I'd never see you again."

"We can't be lucky all our lives," Garrett quipped sourly. "I can't discuss it here. Let's go to my car."

We went downstairs and across the rue Cambon lobby of Le Crebillon—Garrett erect as a trooper, me slinking in my borrowed raincoat. Once we were inside Garrett's car he said to me, "I hate doing this. I really hate it. But I cannot spare a person to make the pickup in Rome. And the statuette must leave Rome by tomorrow morning. The timetable is too tight."

"I'll do it," I said, not waiting to hear more. "I won't even ask what's in the package."

"Why should you?" Garrett said, arching his brows. "You already know what's in it." He turned off the avenue we were driving along and across a bridge, toward the other side of the Seine. I asked him where we were going.

"To Orly airport, of course," he said. "Your flight leaves in an hour."

"But I can't go anywhere dressed like this," I protested, indicating my rumpled dress and borrowed raincoat. Garrett waved my protest aside.

"You have ample funds, Ms. Fein," he said. "Buy yourself a new outfit in Rome. And when you do, make sure you have the raincoat sent back to the US Embassy here in Paris. My cipher clerk doesn't make in a year what you've been given for pin money on this mission."

I let the remark about money slide. "But how will all this take place?" I asked. "How and where do I pick up the figure?"

"All taken care of," Garrett said, handing me an envelope from his coat pocket. "You have detailed instructions on that sheet. Now, I suggest that you spend the balance of our drive to Orly in memorizing the instructions. I'll take back the sheet before you leave."

I did as I was told and, within an hour, I was on board an Alitalia flight for Rome. The plane dipped sharply as it began to circle toward Rome. I caught a glimpse of Paris in the hazy morning sunshine. Despite the warmth of the day, I pulled my borrowed raincoat about me. Then I thought about the owner of that raincoat. Curious, I checked the inside for a label or name tag. Sure enough, there it was, just below the Aquascutum label. It read simply: Gretchen Hinman, 145 rue Daguerre, Paris 14.

I couldn't help but think about Gretchen. She was my size. One feels an affinity for somebody one's own size. Especially if that size isn't a common one. I wondered how old she was, what she was doing at a low-paid diplomatic job in Paris. Still thinking about her, I napped fitfully until we arrived in Rome.

Customs was a breeze. I had nothing with me but my handbag and the clothes I stood in. And while Parisians may be the soul of discretion, I promise you Italian customs officials aren't. As he inspected my passport and asked, *"Dove sono i suoi bagagli?"* I deduced he was asking about my luggage, or lack of it. I have no Italian, except for a few common phrases. Happily, one of them is *"Non capisco Italiano":* I don't speak Italian. I tried it on my customs official, and he understood. He repeated his question in English.

"I have no baggage," I explained.

He gave me a look from head to toe that made me feel as though he were taking off my clothes, item by item. I felt dreadfully uncomfortable under his gaze. Anxious to prevent any misunderstanding, I said, "My baggage was lost by the airlines. In Paris."

"Ma no!" he said, smiling oleaginously. I could see he didn't believe a word. But he finally stamped my passport, and I went on to the main part of the terminal. I was searching for a sign indicating where taxis could be got when I was suddenly pinched firmly, but not painfully, on the behind! I whirled to find the offender, but saw only a sea of faces and figures, all intent on catching or meeting flights. I'd heard that Roman men are fanny patters and pinchers but, until it happened to me, I didn't accept the fact. I still can't, really. What a low opinion Italian men must have of all women, to treat them that way! Just as I caught sight of an exit door marked TAXI, it happened. I was tapped on the shoulder.

True, the touch was a good distance from where I'd been pinched. But I'd had enough personal liberties taken. I whirled and, with my bag in hand, was ready to clobber this offender. I was taken back when I found myself nose to nose with a strange man wearing an apologetic look and a white linen suit.

He was exactly my height, and I'd judge our weights were the same as well. His hairline was somewhere between receding and full retreat, but it was his eyes that were most arresting. Like poached

eggs on either side of his nose, those eyes were re-
garding me from their soft liquid depths with a gaze
I'd last seen on a cocker spaniel.

"Mademoiselle Fein?" he inquired in a soft,
breathy voice. I lowered my bag.

"I am Doris Fein," I said.

"Demeter," said the little sad-eyed man. He was
"one of ours."

"Ceres," I replied dutifully, and watched him
break into a charming, almost boyish smile, so out of
place on that sad face set atop his middle-aged body.

"Welcome to Rome, Ms. Fein," he said, extending
his hand. I suddenly became aware that in my left
hand I still held my handbag, poised to strike a
Roman fanny pincher. As I'm left-handed, I lowered
my weapon as unobtrusively as possible, while shaking his right hand. The little man gave a low-pitched
giggle and said, "You know, mademoiselle, for a moment there, I thought you were going to strike me
with your handbag."

I wasn't about to explain the recent affront to my
dignity and person. So I said, "Sorry. Perhaps I was
overreacting. This is a crucial mission." It was a positive inspiration; I don't know where the idea came
from to say it. But in that one sentence, I had implied
to this man that I was a trained agent, ready to act
if my mission were threatened.

"I understand," the little man with sad eyes said.
He made a courtly gesture as if to say "after you" and
we walked toward a nearby exit. "I have a car wait-

ing for us, Ms. Fein," he said in his peculiar breathy voice.

"I wasn't told I was to be met at the airport," I said. "It's not in my instructions."

"A last-minute change," the little man said, still urging me toward the exit. "You were already on the flight to Rome when I got my orders." Mollified, I accompanied the little man to where a large black sedan was parked. We got in and headed for Rome. The airport is some distance away from the Eternal City.

I saw no point in maintaining any formality, so I rode in the front seat while the little man drove. We swung out of the airport complex and onto a traffic-clogged road that led to Rome. As we drove, the little man said to me, "We haven't exchanged names, have we? Just passwords. I am Pierre Camion."

The man who called himself Camion reached his hand across the front seat of the car, and I took and shook it. His palm was sweaty and a bit clammy. "And you already know my name," I said. "But where are we going? I'm reserved at the Excelsior."

"Yes, I know," said Camion. "But we must make a stop first. There have been some changes in the plan. Changes we could not control. You must receive additional briefing. We are going to a safe house, where you will receive that briefing."

"Drive on, Mr. Camion," I said. But something was puzzling me. My driver, Camion, for all his French name had the traces of a German accent. True, he referred to me as mademoiselle, but that didn't make him French. Any more than his name did. But being new to the spy game, I didn't want to show my ignorance. I *did* know what a safe house was, though. I'd read about safe houses in spy novels. It's a place where you can meet or hide that's unknown to the "other side," whoever they are.

Shortly after we entered the city of Rome itself, I was too engrossed in swiveling my neck and sightseeing to think about my misgivings. Rome was everything I'd expected. If the older parts of Paris were like history come alive, Rome was history with seven capital letters. It seems you can't go four blocks without coming upon some hidden square, each with its own fountain and tiny church. We passed over the Tiber and soon we were in an older area of the city.

For years, I'd read books about Rome, both ancient and modern. I wasn't disappointed. But the traffic—the noise! Somehow, one expects a city as old and steeped in religion as Rome is to be solemn. Far from it. Motor scooters and motorcycles buzzed everywhere, laying down clouds of bluish exhaust. Trucks and cars added their contribution to the morning air until I felt completely at home. The atmosphere was thick enough to qualify as a first-stage smog alert in Los Angeles. As I was musing on the fact that Los Angeles and Rome share one thing, an unbreathable air quality, we pulled up in front of a nondescript house. Camion parked the car on the sidewalk of the narrow street and came around from the driver's side of the black sedan. Sensing that he was about to open the door for me, I forestalled this meaningless act of male courtesy and alit by myself.

Camion guided me up an ill-lit stairway to the second floor of the safe house and once we stood before a massive dark wooden door, he rapped on one panel in a sequence of knocks that had to be code. There was a low click-click-click, indicating an electric door lock release, and Camion pushed the door open. I went into the room, unprepared for what I saw.

Although the exterior of the house was as run-down and ill maintained as any other on this side street, the interior of this room wouldn't have been out of place in a *palazzo*. The floor was carpeted in oriental rugs so luxurious that I hesitated to step into the room. The windows were covered by heavy green velvet drapes that shut out the warm sunlight of the Rome morning. The interior of the room was lighted by a series of wall and floor lamps, each of which could have been a work of art, and probably was.

The walls were dark paneled wood, relieved in their sobriety by an incredible collection of French Impressionist paintings. The furniture was Italian Renaissance, except for a huge leather chair that sat alongside a low carved table that held a water carafe, some glasses of venetian crystal, and a bottle of cognac on a tray. There were also a box of cigars—the label read *Upmann Specials*—several magazines, none of them Italian, and a cigarette box. As I entered the room with Pierre Camion behind me, the occupant of the chair rose to greet me.

He was a ponderously fat man, and it obviously cost him some effort to heave all that bulk into a standing position. He had all the charm of a large pink Jell-O mold. His face, made cherubic by its layers of fat beneath the skin, was arranged in a smile, revealing even, small teeth. The smile caused not a double, but easily a quadruple chin that disappeared into the wing-collared shirt he wore only after several more rolls of flesh hung over its edges.

He was nearly bald, with a fringe of white hair that barely covered the sides of his massive head. Clad in a white linen suit, he resembled nothing more than a pink elephant somehow entangled in a pile of laundry. As he moved, the suit arranged itself in a network of wrinkles that shifted and shook, betraying the gelatinous globus that was his body beneath the folds of white linen. His eyes twinkled merrily as he approached me.

"Buon giorno, Ms. Fein," he said with enthusiasm and extended a hand that looked like a piglet with fingers. "Welcome to Roma! I am Gaspar Viscera!"

Still holding my hand, Viscera guided me to the center of the room. There was a small stuffed armchair alongside the massive leather one at the table. He casually picked it up by its back and set it vis-à-vis the large one. It gave me pause. The chair must have weighed forty pounds, but he picked it up as though it were a feather. There was immense physical strength in that flabby frame. I sat in the armchair as he eased his immense corpus into the oversized leather chair, which groaned its protest as he settled into it.

"A drink, Ms. Fein?" he asked, indicating the brandy bottle on the table. "I would offer you a cigar, were this an all-male meeting. However, these are Macedonian and quite fine," he said, opening the rosewood box to display some cigarettes with gold paper tips.

"Thank you, no," I said, sitting down. "I don't smoke or drink." It wasn't true. Occasionally, I will have some wine, but cognac always tastes like medicine to me. I just don't like the taste.

"Admirable, Ms. Fein," he said. "I'd distrust someone your age who drank. Especially so early in the day." He took a linen handkerchief from his breast pocket and dabbed at his face. The room wasn't all that warm, but I could see small dots of perspiration across the bridge of his nose. "Then shall we get right to our business? That's what we're here for, isn't it?"

"I'm here for additional briefing; if that's the business you mean," I said. "I'm expected to be at the Excelsior Hotel to receive a call." This was true enough. My instructions from Cody Garrett had been to check in and wait in the room for a call from my contact.

Gaspar Viscera poured a few ounces of cognac into one of the glasses on the table.

"Here's to a speedy and profitable resolution to our

mutual problems," he said, raising the glass. I nodded, not knowing what he meant about problems. But I realized that this huge man was a talker, and I couldn't hurry him. I've heard that Europeans consider it rude to jump right into talking business. I thought perhaps I'd offended him, so I let him take his time in coming to his point.

Gaspar Viscera took a cigar from the box on the table and, with a gold cigar cutter that hung from a chain across the massive expanse of his waistcoat, guillotined one end of an Upmann Special. He lit the cigar with a gold lighter from his coat pocket. He inhaled and then emitted a cloud of blue smoke that bespoke the size of his lungs.

"Now, to our business, Ms. Fein," he said, beaming.

"Swell," I said, irked by his snail's pace. "Let's get this over with."

"Marvelous!" he chortled. "We'll get right to the heart of the matter, eh?" He leaned forward toward me, and suddenly his blue eyes were no longer merry. They were hard bits of lapis lazuli, with reddish glints in their centers. "Who has the last figurine, Ms. Fein? And where are you supposed to pick it up?" he rumbled ominously.

"You know all that," I said. "If Mr. Camion knew the password, and he works for you, you should know all there is to know. If you don't . . ." It suddenly sank in on me.

"Then we are not of the IGO," concluded Gaspar Viscera. "Quite right, Ms. Fein. We are not. But you haven't answered my questions, have you?"

I jumped to my feet. As I did, I heard a metallic click from behind me. I spun around and saw Pierre Camion not five feet from the back of my chair. In his hand was a wicked-looking switchblade knife that seemed a foot long!

7

Suddenly, Pierre Camion didn't look like a cocker spaniel. The same wistful smile he'd worn now had taken on a different quality. It was as though he smiled while looking forward to using the long knife he held. He advanced toward me holding the wicked blade in a casual, almost effeminate manner.

"I do so hope you will cooperate, Ms. Fein," Gaspar Viscera oozed. "Pierre has such a lurid imagination when it comes to extracting information from the unwilling."

"But I don't know anything!" I protested. "I was told to check into the Excelsior and await instructions. That's all!"

Viscera didn't answer. He nodded at Camion, who rapidly crossed the room. I got halfway out of my chair before he grabbed me. Here it comes, I thought. My mind flashed back to my adventure in New York, only weeks ago. Carl Suzuki had told me that doing any job for the IGO was dangerous. And acting alone was most dangerous of all—that I shouldn't expect any last-minute rescue. That's for movies, novels, and plays. As Bertolt Brecht says in *The Threepenny Opera*, "The Queen's messenger never comes"—not in real life.

I let out a squeak as Camion grabbed the hair on my head and pulled hard. My neck was roughly drawn across the back of the chair, with my face toward the ceiling. In a bizarre distortion of perspective, all I could see was Camion's face, upside down, his oily smile becoming a grimace, and the sharp edge of the knife as it approached my throat. Ironically, I noted the ceiling of the room for the first time. The motif was of cherubs. A foreshadowing?

"For the last time, Ms. Fein," Viscera said, "where is the last figurine? I assure you, Pierre enjoys his work. Oh, he won't just slit your throat like a chicken's, my dear. He will do it oh, so slowly. You will feel your life seep from your body as the blood flows."

I could barely speak, my throat was constricted by my ungainly posture across the chair back. "I don't know anything, yet," I said weakly.

"Unfortunate, Ms. Fein," Viscera said easily, "your attitude leaves much to be desired. I shall count to three. If by that time you do not tell us the location of the last figurine, you shall surely die. One!"

Tears began to come to my eyes. I thought of home, I thought of my parents. "Two!" Viscera said. I thought of Larry Small and Carl Suzuki. I said a silent prayer. As Gaspar Viscera cried, "Three!" I'm afraid the last word I cried out was "Mommy!"

Suddenly, the fat man said, "Very well, Camion. Release her. She obviously knows nothing." The little man let go of my hair, and I slumped forward in the chair, crying helplessly.

Viscera got to his feet and crossed to where I was sitting and sobbing uncontrollably. He reached into his breast pocket and withdrew the linen handkerchief, which he handed to me.

"A thousand pardons, my dear Ms. Fein," he said. And with this, the globulous monster actually smiled! He continued, "We had to make sure that you truly did not know the whereabouts of the little cossack. I find that at death's door, few people are prepared to lie. No matter how noble the cause."

"But I told you!" I sobbed. "I told you all I knew!" I was mortified. I'd spilled my guts without so much as a nick from the evil blade Pierre Camion still held in his hand. Carl Suzuki was right. I wasn't cut out for this work. Sure, it had seemed a lark when I took it on. And there was patriotism. Some spy I'd turned out to be!

"I sense the cause of your distress, Ms. Fein," said Viscera, taking back his handkerchief. "You feel you would have betrayed anyone or any country to avoid Pierre's knife." He patted my shoulder, and I shrank from his touch. "If it's a consolation to you, my dear," he continued, "better men than I have become babbling fools in Pierre's presence. He can be most persuasive. I think it's because he so obviously enjoys his work. Don't you, Pierre?"

"I follow orders," Camion said from behind me.

"Ah yes," smiled Viscera. "An old song, well sung. I must explain," he said, returning to his chair. He poured out a stiff shot of cognac and handed it to me. I took it without realizing what I was doing. I was mainly concerned with not spilling the drink, not with its contents. My body was quivering all over in spasms of delayed reaction. I tossed off the contents of the glass and nearly choked to death! It was like liquid fire going all the way down. But I must admit that once it reached my stomach, a wave of warmth spread throughout my chest and the tremors stopped. Viscera continued, "You see, Pierre refined his art at Buchenwald when he was just a seventeen-year-old. But there's no denying his talent. Tongues wag at both ends after a few private moments with Pierre."

"I can believe that," I said moistly.

"Excellent," said Viscera, bringing his hands together. He looked like an obscenely evil Buddha. "Now that we understand each other, we can proceed. I had so hoped that you knew the whereabouts of the last figurine. But as you don't, we must improvise. You will do as you were told. You will proceed to the Excelsior Hotel and await instructions. But with one difference. Pierre here will go with you."

Viscera poured out another drink of cognac and drained it. He got to his feet and started for the door of the room. Halfway there, he turned to me and said, "I trust you won't do anything uncooperative, my dear. If you do, or try to warn the IGO . . . well, you have seen the excellent Monsieur Camion in action, haven't you? And now, Ms. Fein, adieu. I have business elsewhere. I leave you to Pierre's tender attentions."

Viscera waddled out the door and closed it without so much as a click from the lock. For a man of his immense bulk, he moved almost soundlessly. I was left in the room alone with Camion, who came around from the back of the chair and extended his hand toward me. I couldn't help it; I flinched. A sorrowful look came over the little fiend's face.

"Oh, please, Ms. Fein," he said softly. "Don't be afraid of me. I am not a bad fellow. But this is an unpleasant world, full of many ugly things. One does what he must to stay alive. I, for instance."

I found some of my recently departed courage. "Don't come near me, you monster!" I snarled. "You would have killed me on the spot. And enjoyed it, too!"

"What is pleasure?" Camion said. "For you, it may be the arms of your friend Fitzroi." I sat bolt upright. So "Claude" was part of their gang! Camion continued in his quiet breathy voice. "For me, it is the sweetness of the relationship between myself and the person I interrogate. In the end, after enough time, my clients, those I question, actually thank me for the release of death. The end to all the ugliness of life. I recall one woman, years ago. She kissed my hand as she died."

I am not given to rough language. Oh, once in a while, a second-degree heckydarn. But I couldn't help what I said. It popped out. "I'll bet she did, you slimy little bastard," I rapped.

"Please, Ms. Fein," Camion said, shrugging his shoulders and smiling. "Let's not have unpleasantness or name calling. Monsieur Viscera has told me I may not kill you . . . now. But he specified nothing as to what condition you will be in. I can keep you alive and conscious while inflicting the most exquisite pain. So let's be nice to each other, shall we?"

I swallowed hard and shuddered. I think what was most chilling was the way Camion used the word *nice*. It's such a Sunday school word, *nice*. One expects the face of evil to be hideous, as in the jiggling obscenity of Gaspar Viscera. But the sad-eyed little man with the cocker spaniel eyes was infinitely more terrifying. I suppose because he didn't look like he could harm anyone or anything.

I ignored the hand Camion extended to help me up from the chair. I stood and looked him in the eye. "Can we leave here now?" I asked.

"Most certainly, Mademoiselle Fein." Camion sighed. "We must be at the Hotel Excelsior for your telephone message, mustn't we?"

I nearly jumped out of my skin when the phone rang in my suite at the Excelsior. I had been sitting staring at the phone since I'd first checked in, with Camion at my side. I was hoping against hope that someone from the IGO would spot us, but I remembered Cody Garrett's words. No one at the Rome bureau knew of my mission. There would be no

Queen's messenger. My thoughts were hopelessly disordered. I knew this hideous little chap was familiar with the passwords Demeter and Ceres. I couldn't tip off my caller without Camion's becoming aware of it. And if he did . . . that knife. That awful knife! I picked up the phone, and Camion picked up the extra earpiece that many continental European phones have. It allows a third person to monitor the telephone conversation.

"Doris Fein here," I said into the mouthpiece.

"Demeter," said a voice. A man's voice.

"Ceres," I replied, disgusted. I was disgusted at myself for being such a coward, and at the IGO for being so sloppy. Viscera, Camion, and Fitzroi knew all the drill and catch phrases.

"You will proceed to the Colosseum at midnight," the telephone voice said. Just a second. There was something familiar about this voice. But the instructions continued: "The Colosseum is closed to tourists. You will find an unbarricaded entrance on its north side, off the Via degli Annabaldi. Once inside, you will go to the center of the arena itself and wait. The moon is full tonight. You will be seen by our contact man. Once he is satisfied you are alone, he will ask for the password. The password is now Romanov. Your countersign will be the word Fabergé. The contact will then hand you a parcel. The parcel will contain a sealed package and an airline ticket to London. Once you have secured the parcel, you will take BA flight 206 to London at six in the morning from

Rome. You will check into the Hyde Park Hotel. Await a message there." There was a click and the line went dead. I heard another small click and, to my horror, saw its source. While I had spoken, Camion had taken no chances on my tipping off the caller. He'd silently eased open his switchblade knife and, once he was satisfied I wasn't going to tip off the IGO, had snapped off the release and folded the blade up again!

Camion glanced at a gold Rolex wristwatch as he folded the blade. "That gives us eight and one half hours before this affair ends," he said, smiling. He reached inside his coat pocket and took out a small vial of black and white capsules. "I don't wish to spend that much time paying attention to you, Ms. Fein. You will take one of these capsules now."

"Poisoned," I said. "You have the information you want, and don't need me anymore. No! I won't take it!"

A look of infinite sadness came over Camion's face. "You wound me, Mademoiselle Fein," Camion said. "Your instructions are quite explicit. And the contact will give the parcel to no one but you. I assure you, this is just a sleeping agent; nothing more. Of course, if you prefer, I can tie and gag you. . . ."

I took the pill; the room spun around almost immediately, and I fell into a pool of ink that also spun and hummed. . . .

I was in a grand ballroom. Crystal chandeliers winked and a full orchestra was playing the *Valse*

Triste of Sibelius. I was waltzing with Claude Fitzroi as the music swirled. The room was lined with mirrors, making an endless perspective of the great ballroom. I caught a glimpse of myself and Claude as we danced.

I was dressed in a full-length formal ball gown of turquoise silk. On my head was a diamond tiara and about my neck a lavalier of emeralds and diamonds that caught the light. Claude was resplendent in a hussar's uniform, with his cape-like coat draped over one shoulder, a dress sword at his side.

"Would your majesty care for some champagne?" Claude asked.

"No, no," I twittered, hating myself as I did. But all I was doing seemed preprogrammed. The words I spoke were scarcely my own. We danced as two figures on an Austrian music box, a moment of grace and beauty, frozen forever in a time long past. I found myself saying, "What is champagne to an evening with the handsomest man in all the Russias? Dance, my dearest, dance!"

Round and round we swirled, ever faster. The faces of the noblemen and women that formed a respectful ring about us on the dance floor began to blur and mix together. Still faster we waltzed. My head spun. "Stop! Stop!" I cried. "I can't breathe!"

"What is breath? What is life?" said Claude fervently as he held me closer. "For this moment, I should gladly die, knowing that just once I held Catherine of Russia in my frightened arms! O Death, take me now! I go with joy in my heart!"

Still faster we danced, the music from the orchestra accelerating until it became distorted, screaming and whining ever faster like a long-playing record suddenly turning at seventy-eight revolutions per minute. The lights and room spun. Claude's face came closer to mine, blotting out my view. I felt the first brush of his lips and he said,

"Wake up, Ms. Fein. It is time."

My eyes flew open and I saw not Claude Fitzroi, but the moon face of Pierre Camion, not inches from mine. I let out a yelp as the memories of the horrid time in Viscera's house came rushing back. In an instant, the little man had clamped his hand over my mouth and nose, cutting off any sound and incidentally any breathing on my part.

"Don't be alarmed," he oiled. "And make no outcry. It is time for us to leave for the Colosseum. Remember, if you make any attempt to warn the contact, you are a dead woman!"

spot where I was standing. I heard the soft *r* he used in pronouncing the password. His accent was Italian. Then before I realized what I was doing, I found my voice.

"Mayday! Mayday!" I screamed and fell to the dusty floor of the ancient arena. Silly of me, I guess. I don't know where I got "Mayday!" from. I know it's an international distress signal, like S.O.S. As I dropped to the floor, I prayed that the courier would do the same, seeing what I did. I heard a muffled *pop* from the shadows behind me, and saw the courier stop, then reel. In the bright moonlight, I saw the look of shock on his face. I scrambled to my feet and began running. I caught the parcel he held before it fell to the ground from his already lifeless fingers. I zigzagged to my right.

Another *pop!* A puff of dust sprang up from the floor, inches in front of me, and where I would have been had I not zigzagged. I reversed direction and made for the concealment of the shadowed galleries. I had almost made it when a big chunk of rock exploded inches from my face. I felt a stinging sensation as I was sprayed across the face by flying rock fragments. But by then, I was past the galleries and into the blessed darkness.

Though most of the Colosseum was visible in the full moon, once I was in the shadows it was positively Stygian. I ran, unheeding. I hit my shins hard against a low outcropping of stone and fell heavily. It knocked the wind out of me. I lay there for a second,

8

One hears of seeing the Colosseum by moonlight, as much as the Acropolis in Athens. Any other time, I would have been enchanted by the prospect. I didn't feel that way now, standing alone in the center of the arena, the scene of so many deaths and agonies in the past. In fact, my primary concern was not becoming another victim in the long list of those who had perished here.

I wish that I could say my mind was filled with plans for warning the courier who was to give me the parcel. It wasn't. All I could think of was Pierre Camion. Just before I walked alone into the center of the moonlit arena, he had folded the knife he carried and produced instead a nasty automatic pistol with a silencer attached.

"I am a superb shot, Mademoiselle Fein," he said. "I will be holding you in my sights each second you stand out there. If in any way you attempt to abort this delivery, the first shot I fire will kill the courier. The second will enter your body at mid-spine. If you live, which I doubt, you will be hopelessly paralyzed for life. Considering your age, death would be more pleasant than a lifetime as a cripple, don't you think?"

He didn't really expect an answer; I gave none. I swallowed what had to be my heart and nodded acquiescence. Camion consulted his Rolex; it was visible in the moon-washed ruins of the Colosseum. "It is time," he said, and nudged the small of my back with the silencer end of the pistol. Mind ajumble, knees shaking, I walked alone into the center of the arena. I stood there for a few seconds before I thought I saw a movement from the shadowed galleries that line the arena floor. It *was* a movement!

I watched ineffectively as the courier approached where I stood. What to do? The messenger, a parcel visible in his hand, was almost out of the shadows and into the bright moonlight of the arena. He was a short man, taller than Cody Garrett but, as I've pointed out, that doesn't take much. *I'm* taller than Garrett. I could see that the courier wasn't too much older than I, and dressed in the uniform most European young people have adopted: blue jeans, sneakers, and a decorated T-shirt. Incongruously, the T-shirt he wore was imprinted with the tongue-out logo of the Rolling Stones. As I said, I wasn't thinking of any heroic act. I was too frightened for that. But the thought of Pierre Camion in the shadows, gun aimed, was suddenly supplanted in my mind by something that had happened years ago.

My grandfather Fein had told me on the occasion of my fifteenth birthday about the meaning of the Feast of Chanukkah. Not that I didn't already know about Judah Maccabee, "The Hammer of God." I was

raised on those stories. But Grandpa would al retell it. It was a family ritual.

"As a Jew, Doris," he had said, "you must a remember our people's proud history of fig against tyrants and oppressors. As Judah Mac fought against the tyranny of the Greeks, so m fight tyrants everywhere today. For as long as fight tyrants everywhere today. For as long as exist, no people are ever safe. They will alw in fear of the knock at the door in the night; the safety of their families and their human

"But Grandpa," I'd said, "I'm only one per not a soldier, either."

He took my face between both his hands with frightening intensity, "So was Esther ling. But she saved her people from the t Haman. And she risked her power, positic to do it. Can you do less?"

As the courier approached me, lookin and defenseless in that silly Rolling Sto my grandfather's words took on new mea I thought of Camion, hiding in the shad evil thing of darkness he was. I thought he'd struck in my deepest soul and, wasn't frightened anymore. I was angr than that. I was hopping mad!

The courier with the parcel was n splash of moonlight, not six meters a that had me rooted was suddenly br my mouth to speak, but at first nothi out. "Romanov," said the courier as

8

One hears of seeing the Colosseum by moonlight, as much as the Acropolis in Athens. Any other time, I would have been enchanted by the prospect. I didn't feel that way now, standing alone in the center of the arena, the scene of so many deaths and agonies in the past. In fact, my primary concern was not becoming another victim in the long list of those who had perished here.

I wish that I could say my mind was filled with plans for warning the courier who was to give me the parcel. It wasn't. All I could think of was Pierre Camion. Just before I walked alone into the center of the moonlit arena, he had folded the knife he carried and produced instead a nasty automatic pistol with a silencer attached.

"I am a superb shot, Mademoiselle Fein," he said. "I will be holding you in my sights each second you stand out there. If in any way you attempt to abort this delivery, the first shot I fire will kill the courier. The second will enter your body at mid-spine. If you live, which I doubt, you will be hopelessly paralyzed for life. Considering your age, death would be more pleasant than a lifetime as a cripple, don't you think?"

He didn't really expect an answer; I gave none. I swallowed what had to be my heart and nodded acquiescence. Camion consulted his Rolex; it was visible in the moon-washed ruins of the Colosseum. "It is time," he said, and nudged the small of my back with the silencer end of the pistol. Mind ajumble, knees shaking, I walked alone into the center of the arena. I stood there for a few seconds before I thought I saw a movement from the shadowed galleries that line the arena floor. It *was* a movement!

I watched ineffectively as the courier approached where I stood. What to do? The messenger, a parcel visible in his hand, was almost out of the shadows and into the bright moonlight of the arena. He was a short man, taller than Cody Garrett but, as I've pointed out, that doesn't take much. *I'm* taller than Garrett. I could see that the courier wasn't too much older than I, and dressed in the uniform most European young people have adopted: blue jeans, sneakers, and a decorated T-shirt. Incongruously, the T-shirt he wore was imprinted with the tongue-out logo of the Rolling Stones. As I said, I wasn't thinking of any heroic act. I was too frightened for that. But the thought of Pierre Camion in the shadows, gun aimed, was suddenly supplanted in my mind by something that had happened years ago.

My grandfather Fein had told me on the occasion of my fifteenth birthday about the meaning of the Feast of Chanukkah. Not that I didn't already know about Judah Maccabee, "The Hammer of God." I was raised on those stories. But Grandpa would always retell it. It was a family ritual.

"As a Jew, Doris," he had said, "you must always remember our people's proud history of fighting against tyrants and oppressors. As Judah Maccabee fought against the tyranny of the Greeks, so must we fight tyrants everywhere today. For as long as tyrants exist, no people are ever safe. They will always live in fear of the knock at the door in the night; fear for the safety of their families and their human rights."

"But Grandpa," I'd said, "I'm only one person. And not a soldier, either."

He took my face between both his hands and said with frightening intensity, "So was Esther, my darling. But she saved her people from the tyranny of Haman. And she risked her power, position, and life to do it. Can you do less?"

As the courier approached me, looking so young and defenseless in that silly Rolling Stones T-shirt, my grandfather's words took on new meaning to me. I thought of Camion, hiding in the shadows like the evil thing of darkness he was. I thought of the terror he'd struck in my deepest soul and, suddenly, I wasn't frightened anymore. I was angry. I was more than that. I was hopping mad!

The courier with the parcel was now in the full splash of moonlight, not six meters away. The spell that had me rooted was suddenly broken. I opened my mouth to speak, but at first nothing would come out. "Romanov," said the courier as he neared the spot where I was standing. I heard the soft *r* he used in pronouncing the password. His accent was Italian. Then before I realized what I was doing, I found my voice.

"Mayday! Mayday!" I screamed and fell to the dusty floor of the ancient arena. Silly of me, I guess. I don't know where I got "Mayday!" from. I know it's an international distress signal, like S.O.S. As I dropped to the floor, I prayed that the courier would do the same, seeing what I did. I heard a muffled *pop* from the shadows behind me, and saw the courier stop, then reel. In the bright moonlight, I saw the look of shock on his face. I scrambled to my feet and began running. I caught the parcel he held before it fell to the ground from his already lifeless fingers. I zigzagged to my right.

Another *pop!* A puff of dust sprang up from the floor, inches in front of me, and where I would have been had I not zigzagged. I reversed direction and made for the concealment of the shadowed galleries. I had almost made it when a big chunk of rock exploded inches from my face. I felt a stinging sensation as I was sprayed across the face by flying rock fragments. But by then, I was past the galleries and into the blessed darkness.

Though most of the Colosseum was visible in the full moon, once I was in the shadows it was positively Stygian. I ran, unheeding. I hit my shins hard against a low outcropping of stone and fell heavily. It knocked the wind out of me. I lay there for a second, hearing only the breath whistling in and out of my lungs and the pounding of my heart. Then to my utter horror, I heard the soft scraping that meant footsteps. It was Camion, searching me out in the darkness. To complete my terror, I heard the nasty *click* as he pushed the button that opened the blade of that knife he wielded. I knew that's what it was; once having heard that sound, I'd never forget it. The little monster was stalking me!

I got to my feet as silently as I could. I knew he had to be close by for me to hear the knife open that way. I began to move toward the higher galleries, keeping my head and upper body low and in the shadows. I hadn't gone a few meters when I tripped and fell again. The blow to my already raw shins was so sharp and abrupt that I couldn't help it; I let out a gasp of shock and pain.

As I started to get to my feet again, I could hear Camion's footsteps coming my way, much faster. I reached out to my left, expecting to find the low outcropping of stone that formed each side of the galleries. To my shock, it wasn't there. I rolled to one side and dropped through a hole in the gallery, a distance of only four feet, but the complete surprise of it stunned me for a second.

As I regained my wits, I felt about me and discovered that I was inside a niche roughly the dimensions of a coffin. It was a space below the level of the gallery. Then I saw a flickering light in the darkness above me! As I watched, too petrified with fear to emit a squeak, the light came closer and closer. Finally, it cast a dim puddle of light right above where I stood!

I glanced up and found myself looking directly at Camion's diminutive body from the feet to the knees. I noted with satisfaction that Camion had evidently tripped in the darkness, too. There were two soiled spots on the knees of his white linen suit. He was wearing two-toned black and white shoes, and I noticed that the heels of his shoes were built up, to give him more height. The thought of that horrible little man wearing lifts on his shoes to salve his vanity suddenly struck me as comical. Don't ask me why, but I had an absurd impulse to giggle. It had to be hysteria.

Abruptly, I heard a scraping noise from somewhere above me and over to my left. Camion heard it too, and the view I had of his shoes disappeared as he extinguished the flickering light. He had to be lighting matches to see in the blackness of the galleries. I heard his self-consciously softened footsteps recede into the darkness.

I don't know how long I stayed there in that grave-sized hole in the stands. It seemed an eternity. Finally, when I heard no sounds at all, I eased myself back up to the level of the gallery I had fallen from. I poked my head up above the level of the gallery and surveyed the center of the arena. It was deserted. Only the unmoving form of the courier, spread-eagled on the Colosseum floor, remained.

Then, it moved! The courier was still alive!

He emitted a low moan and rolled over on his side. Like an evil spider, attracted by vibrations in its web, I saw the figure of Camion, his suit badly soiled and torn, emerge from the shadows for a second, then retreat. He was waiting there like a hunter, using the wounded courier for bait. He evidently hoped that if I heard the courier, I would try to help.

Truthfully, I was torn. I wanted to help the fallen agent but, if I went anywhere near the center of the Colosseum, Camion would pounce. The only bit of luck in my situation was that Camion was on the far side of the arena. The entrance through which we'd come was on my side. I say luck because I frankly didn't know where any of the other exits were, or if they were barricaded. Abandoning discretion and ignoring my trembling knees, I dashed across the near corner of the arena, momentarily exposing myself, then I was again in darkness, running for all I was worth.

I heard the pounding of footfalls echoing behind me. I ran even faster . . . faster than I ever knew I could. I banged and clattered off the sides of the narrow corridor that led to the entrance. Then, suddenly, I was outside in the bright lights of Rome at midnight. All around me, traffic swirled on the busy Via degli Annabaldi. I looked over my shoulder and, to my dismay, saw Camion burst from the shadows, too. He stopped suddenly, realizing he still held his open-bladed knife and, while he closed it, I dashed right out into traffic, waving frantically at cars, praying that one would stop. Fat chance.

The cars eddying about me as I waved whizzed by without even reducing speed. I saw the face of one female driver as she sped by and from her expression deduced that I wasn't the sort of hitchhiker anyone would have stopped for. I knew I must look a horrendous sight: torn hose, filthy clothes from the falls I'd taken in the darkened Colosseum.

Then I saw a taxicab! Or I should say the driver saw me. I'd been looking *across* the Via degli Annabaldi. This cab had evidently been parked on the darker side of the thoroughfare. The driver flashed his headlights and sounded his horn. I'd never seen such a welcome sight in my life.

Ignoring the cars that actually brushed against the flapping coattails of my borrowed raincoat, I grabbed the rear door handle of the cab as it pulled up alongside me and hurled myself into the back seat. Desperately trying to piece together some Italian I said, *"Aeroporto di Roma . . . presto . . . presto!"*

The cabdriver must have understood my pidgin Italian, because without so much as turning to look at his passenger (I was grateful for that), he slammed the car into gear, and the Fiat jumped into traffic like a goosed antelope. I saw the expression of frustration and anger on Camion's face as I peered out the cab's back window at the rapidly receding bulk of the Colosseum.

We were in the mainstream of traffic now, and

moving fast. I sat back in the narrow seat of the minicab and heaved an immense sigh of relief. As I did, I finally remembered the name I had been searching my mind for. The airport for Rome is called *aeroporto Leonardo Da Vinci.* Of all the unforgettable names to forget! Trying to appear more cosmopolitan, I formulated a sentence in my broken Italian. I wanted to say, "How long will it take to the airport?" but I didn't know how. The best I could muster was, "Is it far to the airport?" I leaned forward and said to the back of the driver's head, *"É lontano all' aeroporto Leonardo Da Vinci?"*

"Non é lontano, signorina," said the driver. Then, to my amazement, he added in English, "And most people in Rome don't call it that. They call it 'Fiumicino,' Doris." As he spoke, he half turned toward the backseat where I was leaning forward. At the same instant, we passed under some brilliant street lighting, and I saw the face of my rescuer/driver. It was none other than my recently suave escort in Paris, Claude Fitzroi!

I immediately grabbed at the door handle of the cab but, as though he sensed I would do it, Claude tramped down on the gas pedal of the little cab, and we were soon hurtling down the broad avenue at a breakneck pace. I know that you might expect this to be a maneuver that would attract police. I hoped it would. I was ready to tell my story to Roman authorities, and IGO security be hanged. I had eluded Pierre Camion only to run right into the arms, so to speak, of another member of Gaspar Viscera's vicious gang!

But I'd reckoned without the normal pace of Roman traffic. It seems that anyone behind the wheel of an automobile in Rome automatically becomes possessed of a profound death wish. As headlong as Claude's speed seemed to be, it was actually matched or exceeded by other vehicles on the streets! I would have taken a chance and even jumped from the moving cab, as I had jumped from the moving ambulance in New York, weeks ago. But to do so in a jam of traffic thick as a parking lot and moving bumper to bumper at forty-five miles an hour would have been surer death than taking my chances with Pierre Camion in a darkened Colosseum!

Fitzroi drove at the same headlong pace until we were well outside Roman traffic patterns. Then he pulled over to the side of the road and, before I could attempt to get out and run, had flung open the back door and grabbed me by the wrist. His grip was not friendly. It hurt.

"You're hurting my wrist," I protested.

"I'll do more than that if you don't do exactly as I tell you," said Claude grimly. "This is too important for you to mess up with amateur heroics."

Suddenly, the events of the past two-and-a-half days hit me hard. It was as though someone had let all the air out of a balloon. I'd been in deadly peril twice in the past twelve hours, had a knife so close to my throat that I felt its edge. I'd been bullied, threatened, and physically abused. "All right," I said with resignation. "I won't run. I won't cry out."

"That's a sensible girl." Claude smiled. "Cooperate, and you may yet get out of this in one piece."

"Don't you condescend to me, you phony!" I snapped. "I'm no girl. I'm a woman, and my own person! If I could, I'd break you to pieces with my own two hands!"

"My, my, aren't we bloodthirsty?" he said in that French accent, which I no longer found charming. "Now, get into the front seat," he ordered.

I got inside and, as I did so, my phony Fitzroi produced a pair of handcuffs. He quickly manacled my left wrist to the grab iron that grew out of the dashboard on the passenger side of the Fiat's front seat. The sneaky bastard even remembered from our night on the town in Paris that I'm left-handed. He returned to the driver's seat and started up the car. In seconds we were again speeding through the night.

"Where are we going? To Viscera's?" I asked. "He'll be anxious to get the cossack."

"He certainly will, Doris," Claude said. "But you misunderstand. I don't work for Viscera. I'm an independent contractor. I may do business with him, but I don't like him any better than you do." He glanced over at me. I kept an impassive face. In truth, I didn't believe a word of what he said. "But you have a flight to catch out of Fiumicino at six this morning. That one will be watched by Camion, I'm sure. We'll be taking an earlier flight."

"But why?" I protested. "You have me and the figurine now. And whoever you had rob my room in Paris has the quartz boyar as well. Can't you just let *me* out someplace? I won't tell anyone. Really. Just let me go. I'm of no use to you now." I know it sounded cowardly, but all I could think of was my pending reunion with Pierre Camion and his knife. And what was Claude talking about: avoiding being seen by Camion at six A.M.? What difference did it make if they all worked together? I asked him about this as we drove on.

"Simple." He smiled. "The ultimate customer for the figures is in London. To deliver the two figures I now have—"

"What?" I squeaked. "Two figures?"

"But certainly, two figures," he said. "I now have the quartz boyar and the jade cossack you still have clutched to your breast. But only you can take them through customs unchecked. That was arranged by your employers, the IGO." He saw my look of dismay. "Oh come, come," he continued. "Surely you must have deduced by now that I know all about your bosses. And as surely, you must know that I do not work for Viscera. If he knew I was here in this cab, Camion would be hunting me to get the two figures."

"I don't understand at all," I said.

"It's not too difficult to comprehend, Doris. Gaspar Viscera is an international criminal. But no one has ever been able to prove conclusively that he is. He owns one of the largest import-export businesses in Europe. He moves freely from country to country on his Italian passport, though he's not Italian."

"I thought it was funny," I said. "His accent is more English than anything else."

"He's actually an Albanian," Claude said. "But his Italian citizenship is above reproach. It was a reward the Italian goverment gave him for locating national art treasures hidden by the Fascists during World War II. Though in truth, many people feel it was he who stole and hid them to begin with."

We were now entering the approach to the airport, and Claude began to speak faster. "My relationship with Viscera is one of business, purely. I have the two figures he wants. But to be able to sell them to him, I must arrange a safe transfer. Safe for me, that is. If Viscera knew the location of the figures, there would be no point in paying me for them. He would have Camion slit my throat and save the money. And I'm sure Camion saw me pick you up outside the Colosseum. No, Doris, *chérie,* you are not only my means of getting the statucttes to England. Because you are expected at customs and Italian airports have armed guards, you are also my life insurance."

Claude pulled the cab into a parking space in an unused section of the parking lot. Then once parked, he came around to my side of the car and, after first relieving me of my parcel, unlocked my handcuffs. "I will accompany you through the customs on either side of the flight," he said. "I shall never be more than an arm's reach from you." He grabbed my arm so tightly I winced. "I will be your . . . how do you say it? . . . lover boy. You will appear to be absolutely and foolishly in love with me."

"That's a tall order, you lying sneak."

"I'm sure you will do it well," Claude said firmly. "You see, my life is worthless if I am exposed. There is too much blood on this set of dolls. So, if you cry out, or make any disturbance at either this or the London airport, I will kill you where you stand. I have nothing to lose at this point."

"Whatever you say," I said. But my mind was racing. I knew that Claude couldn't get any weapon past the flight gate barriers. The X-ray machines there would show it immediately. I had to bide my time until we got beyond those barriers.

As if he read my mind, Claude said, "You may wonder just how I can kill you in a place where I can carry no knife or gun. Observe, please." He stepped over to the front end of the Fiat cab and, with a motion so fast I almost didn't see it, brought his right hand chopping down in a karate blow to the hood of the car. His hand passed my face as he did, and I swear I heard the air whistle as it whipped by the point of my nose. There was a hollow *bong* sound and, when I looked again, there was a massive dent two inches deep in the stout steel surface of the car hood.

"The car is made of steel." Fitzroi smiled. "Your

neck, from my delightful experience of last night, is much softer."

I looked at the dent in the car and swallowed hard. Claude may have been prettier than Pierre Camion, but there seemed no doubt he was equally deadly. I shrugged my shoulders in resignation. "Lead on," I said, and arm in arm we walked to the airport main entrance.

London

9

I didn't try to cause a fuss at either the Rome airport or at Heathrow, where we landed. I suppose I could have tried. I had an opportunity, movie style, to scrawl a message on the ladies' room mirror in Rome, where Claude allowed me time to clean up while he stood outside the door. I had been hoping that there would be an attendant there, as there are in Paris. But the hour was late and the room deserted.

Ironically enough, when I came out of the ladies' room, Claude hadn't been standing outside the door after all. He'd been buying a ticket. He was walking toward me from the ticket counters, a folder in his hand. If I had only known I wasn't being watched! But now, it was too late.

And even if there had been an opportunity, there was always the problem of my nearly nonexistent Italian. I didn't even speak with Claude on the flight to London. I brooded. You see, I had learned a lot about myself during those minutes in the moonlit Colosseum.

I am not the stuff of which heroines are made. On the face of it, I may have appeared to have acted bravely. But what had I gained? The courier had been wounded. For all I knew, he was dead by now.

And it seemed to me that, in part, I was responsible. My mind kept flashing back to that instant when the bullet from Camion's pistol had struck him. There was something so very unheroic about dying in the dirt while wearing a Rolling Stones T-shirt!

That memory was bad enough, but it was also very much in my mind that it could have been me! When I'd acted to warn the courier, it had been out of a rage so profound that I'd momentarily forgotten my fear. But now, with my precious self saved at the expense of another, I was secretly glad that the fallen figure on the floor of the Colosseum wasn't Doris Fein. I felt guilty about that, too. That's when I decided that if I ever got out of this mess alive, I was retiring from the heroine business.

Claude wasn't in a talkative mood, either. Once we'd landed at Heathrow, there were a few dicey moments as we passed through customs. Despite my taking an earlier flight than planned, the customs official had the right passwords. The two packages I had in my purse were undisturbed by any inspection.

It may have been an opportunity to cry out, but Claude was immediately behind me in the customs line. As he already knew the passwords, I couldn't tip off the customs guard. Uneventfully, we were allowed to enter Great Britain. We were soon in a cab headed for London.

I had told the driver we wanted the Hyde Park Hotel but, once we were inside London proper, Claude got the driver's attention and began to direct him elsewhere. As to just where we went, I couldn't say. I'd never been to London, and it was still quite dark. I do know that the section we went to is called Belgravia.

From what I could see of the area in the light of street lamps, the section was one of contrasts. It seemed to be a once posh neighborhood that had gone to seed and, in places, was being restored to some of its former elegance. We passed a row of town houses all sparkling with new paint and burnished brass, then a row of identical buildings that were shabby. They looked as though they had been converted into cheap rooming houses. As we passed through this seamy block, Claude had the driver stop in front of a run-down building. Once the driver had been paid, Claude took my elbow in a semipainful grip and guided me around the block.

The house we stopped in front of was neither restored nor neglected. It looked as though it had been reasonably maintained, nothing more. But I knew why Claude had gone through the maneuver. He didn't want the cabdriver who dropped us off to know our real destination. For the first time in hours, Claude spoke to me. "Doris," he said, "you must listen carefully to my instructions. If you don't, you will surely die." Noting my expression, he added, "Oh, not at my hands. In the clutches of your friend Viscera. This is his London headquarters. Or one of them, at any rate. His smuggling activities are based here."

"What's that to me?" I replied dully. "I've been

bullied, frightened, and threatened. I've been lied to by everyone from you to my employers. All I want now is a place to lie down and feel safe. I don't care anymore. What is it you want me to do?"

"That's the attitude, Doris," he said. "Keep cooperating, and you may get your wish. First, I want you to go up those steps and knock at the door."

"And then?"

"That's it. Just stand there. A servant will open the door."

Claude followed me up the steps but, when I was about to use the big brass door knocker, he laid a restraining hand on my forearm. I waited while he plastered himself alongside the doorway, out of sight of anyone who might answer my knock. Then he nodded to me. I rapped hard with the knocker.

After a minute or so, a light came on downstairs and the door swung partly open. I nearly died on the spot. How he got there before us, or how my face must have looked, I couldn't say. But the man who opened the door was Pierre Camion!

I gave a small cry of fear as all the memories of the Colosseum chase came rushing back. Camion reacted almost immediately. He made a grab for me. I, quite naturally, jumped back. My move caused Camion to come partly out of the doorway, which evidently was exactly what Claude had planned on.

As Camion extended a hand to grab me, Claude acted from his hiding place alongside the door. He grabbed Camion's arm in some sort of judo hold and, in a split second, had the odious little man in a one-armed stranglehold.

"Move a muscle, and I'll snap your neck," he growled in Camion's ear. "All I want is an excuse to kill you. Do you understand?"

Camion's poached-egg eyes bugged out even farther. Claude relaxed his grip a trifle. "Yes, *jawohl,*" gurgled Camion through the stranglehold. I had the supreme satisfaction of seeing fear written large on the little rotter's face. I'm a nonviolent person by nature, but I think if Claude had wrung Camion's neck, I would have watched the performance with infinite delight.

Still holding Camion, Claude used his free hand to search through the little man's coat pockets. He promptly extracted a revolver. Having disarmed Camion, Claude pushed the now unarmed man through the doorway, and then did the same with me.

The interior of Viscera's London house, like the one in Rome, bore little resemblance to its exterior. The foyer of the town house was floored in shiny marble tile of black and white. The oriental rug that lay in its center extended to the bottom step of a beautiful staircase that led to the upper floors. But what descended those stairs just as we entered wasn't at all beautiful. It was the bloated bulk of Gaspar Viscera.

His piggish eyes quickly assessed the situation and the pistol that Claude held aimed at him. He arranged his features in a smile that held no mirth. He was wearing black trousers and a shirt open at the throat. On his feet were those old-fashioned soft leather slippers you see people wearing in late movies. To top off the ensemble, he wore a red velvet smoking jacket that made him look like a fire truck that jiggled when it moved.

"Ah, Monsieur Fitzroi and Mademoiselle Fein!" he exclaimed, as if we had just dropped in on a social call. "How very good to see you both again! Do come in." Viscera descended the last step and, once the aftershocks had finished rippling through his body, added, "And do put away that weapon, Monsieur Fitzroi. I am not given to mock heroics, and Camion is quite harmless without a weapon. I assume that it is his pistol you hold, correct?"

"Absolument, Monsieur Viscera," Claude said evenly. "But you *will* forgive me this small formality?" He waved the pistol casually, directing Viscera to stand next to Camion.

"If I must," sighed Viscera with a show of wounded feelings. He turned to Claude once he was a few feet from Camion.

"Please forgive me this outburst, won't you?" he said to Claude, and with the speed of a striking snake, he delivered a full-armed stinging slap to the face of Pierre Camion. In the marble-floored foyer, the slap resounded like a pistol shot. Immediately a red, welted imprint of Viscera's hand sprang to the cheek of Pierre Camion, while the little man reeled from the sheer weight of Viscera's blow.

"You were careless, Pierre," he said to the little man jovially, as though reproaching a child for a minor misconduct. Then he turned to Claude and said, "Sorry. The servant problem, you know. One must maintain discipline with one's underlings. In another time, such a blunder would have cost this insect his life."

"And I, for one, wouldn't have shed a tear," I put in.

Viscera laughed at my remark. It was a deep-seated laugh that began as a half-cough and rumbled up from his elephantine depths, erupting in a series of *ho-ho's* that caused his whole body to shake like a monstrous plate of jelly. It must have been the *ho-ho's,* but suddenly he reminded me of an evil, beardless Santa.

"Excellent sentiments, Ms. Fein," he said to me. "Show your enemies no mercy. Crush them under-foot as you would any vermin!" His piggish face took on a mock-sad look. "But I am a thoughtless host," he oozed. "Do have a drink. Come into my drawing room . . ."

"Said the spider to the fly," I interjected.

"And have the chill taken from your bones with a fine cognac," he added, ignoring my remark. He indicated a set of sliding doors, just off the foyer.

"After you, monsieur," said Claude, waving the pistol. "Have Camion open the doors, turn on the lights, and stand in mid-room. Hands atop his head."

"You are a prudent man, Monsieur Fitzroi," said Viscera, smiling. "I like that in a man. I, too, am prudent. I like to think that although the years have taught me prudence, they have not crippled me with caution." Then, to Camion, "Do as he says, Pierre."

Camion obeyed briskly, and I followed Viscera into the sitting room with Claude and his pistol right behind me. As I did, Viscera grabbed me with the same speed I'd seen him display before, and spun me about to face Claude. From his smoking jacket pocket, he'd drawn a nasty automatic, scarcely bigger than a toy, and held it directly against my temple!

"Lay down your weapon, monsieur," he said, "or I shall surely put a bullet into Ms. Fein's brain!"

To my horror, Claude did nothing of the sort. He went into a light crouch and with a two-handed grip I'd seen only in films, aimed the pistol directly at Viscera behind me!

"She's too small to hide behind, you *idiot*," snapped Claude. "And what if you do kill her? What is that to me? I have the figurines you want. Are we here to do business or play at red Indians, Viscera?"

Abruptly, Viscera released me and broke into his false hearty laugh. He dropped the gun onto the carpeted floor. "It was worth a try, monsieur," he said. He shrugged his massive shoulders and stood clear of me. I whirled in anger to Claude.

"You would have let him kill me!" I accused.

Claude gave a Gallic shrug, smiled sheepishly, and replied, "But he would have died as well, Doris. And what I said is true. Remember that. You are no longer of any use to me. You have transported the figures through customs. Whether you live or die is important only to yourself. If it is important, I should advise you to shut up and sit in that chair while Viscera and I do business." I did as I was told.

Claude directed Viscera and Camion to chairs that sat alongside a low, beautifully inlaid table. He remained standing. The pistol lay where Viscera had dropped it, feet away from where I sat. As though he read my mind, Claude went over and picked up the gun, pocketing it without once taking his eyes off Viscera and Camion.

"I wouldn't tempt you to try something foolish, Doris," he said. He came over to where I sat and took my handbag. I couldn't believe that this was the man who had been so *charmant* in Paris, two days ago. Those lovely blue eyes, half hooded by sooty dark long lashes, were hard as sapphires. "Now to business, monsieur," he said, tossing one of the packages to Viscera, who fielded it as easily as Pete Rose gobbling up a slow grounder.

Viscera's sausage-like fingers quickly ripped away the outer wrapping of the package. For the first time, I actually saw the thing for which I had been kidnapped, lied to, and almost murdered. Viscera noted my expression as he set the little statue on the low table before him. He looked at the diminutive figure with the same gaze Petunia would have given to a double Banana Boat from Baskin-Robbins. The naked lust for the gem-encrusted statuette shone clearly in his piglike eyes. He was almost drooling as he said in a dreamy, faroff voice, "Behold the consummate art of Carl Fabergé! The quartz boyar! Note the beauty of the carving, the perfection of the enamel. The *petits brillants!* The tsars are gone, their follies and pretensions with them. But art, the true art of Fabergé, endures." With quivering jowls, he pointed a finger at the tiny Russian nobleman, caught forever in the act of drawing his lilliputian sword. "Look how the light catches the diamonds on the hilt of his little saber! The exquisite fashioning of his costume. The delicacy of the sapphire eyes. . . . Is it any wonder men have killed and others died to hold such beauty in hand? To be able to say, *This is mine!* Ah, it is worth every act of violence, every drop of blood shed to possess it!"

"You don't own it, Viscera," Claude reminded. "Not until I get my price."

"The other figure," Viscera said, his face and voice unchanged. "You have the other figure?"

Claude flipped the other package to Viscera, who pounced on it like a great pink spider. I watched in disgust as he slobbered over the second statuette, once he'd torn off the wrappings.

"Pink and white jade," he cooed. "Ingeniously joined to a larger piece of purest green jade. A soupçon of black enamel for the little cossack's beard, boots, and hat . . . seed pearls, diamonds, and rubies, all set upon a pedestal of finest filigreed platinum.

Yes, yes, this is a moment!"

His face lost its dreamy look as he tore his eyes from the figure of the cossack and turned his attention to Claude Fitzroi once more. In a voice that sounded like a small boy's asking for a second helping of dessert, he asked, "May I put the figures together, as they should be?"

"As you wish, Viscera. Where are they?"

Viscera looked askance at Claude, who allowed him to stand up. He waddled over to a gorgeous antique armoire of matched grain mahogany that stood against a nearby wall. With elaborate caution, keeping his massive right arm clear of his body, he reached into the breast pocket of his smoking jacket. I was watching Viscera but, from immediately behind me, I heard a *click* as Claude thumbed back the hammer on the revolver. Viscera froze instantly.

"The key," he said, smiling apologetically.

"Very well," Claude answered. "But if there is a gun inside that cabinet, you are a dead man, Viscera."

"No, no," Viscera said hurriedly. "I haven't come so close to my life's ambition to throw away this moment. See for yourself, the mastery of Fabergé!"

Viscera opened the doors of the armoire wide and stood back. There was a small light inside, set to go on when the doors opened, like a refrigerator. The interior of the armoire was lined in mirrors and, when I saw its contents, I couldn't help letting out a small gasp, for in that instant, I realized how little 1 truly knew about this whole mad, violent affair.

Inside the cabinet were twenty-two small figures, each in its own niche of plate glass mirror. The light played over jasper and jade, diamonds and emeralds, coral and porphyry, pearls and opals, rubies and sapphires, gold and platinum. It was breathtaking not only in its beauty, but in the incredible fortune it represented. I was about to comment, but Viscera spoke again.

"May I place them together?" he asked of Claude.

"Whatever you want, Viscera," Claude said evenly. "Once you are done drooling over them, we can talk business."

With trembling hands, Viscera picked up the two figures from the low table and carried them to the armoire. He gently set the quartz boyar and the jade cossack in spaces already reserved for them. Viscera stood with his back to us, and I saw his great body begin to shake. I was prepared for another dozen or so ho-ho-ho's but, when he turned to face us, I saw tears streaming down his face. This wretch, this evil, wicked man, was crying at the beauty of the collection!

"Thirty-five years," he sobbed. "More than half my life, I have waited for this moment. I have traveled tens of thousands of miles, lied, cheated, and murdered. All to the end of this perfect moment!" He reached for his jacket pocket, then froze, remembering Claude's pistol aimed at him. "Forgive me," he said to Claude. "The emotion of the moment. May I get my handkerchief?"

Claude nodded and Viscera withdrew a square of fine linen from his jacket pocket. He blew his nose with a resounding *honk* and dabbed at his streaming eyes. "But now, to business," he said, his voice regaining its normal, oleaginous timbre.

"Two million five," said Claude flatly.

"Dollars," asked Viscera, raising his eyebrows, "or French francs?"

"Neither," Claude replied. *"Swiss* francs. Deposited to my numbered account in Zurich. No, don't bother to protest, *monsieur,* I know that all you need do is pick up a telephone and call Zurich to do it."

"But I am not that rich a man," Viscera protested.

"You have that amount and twenty times more, *cochon,"* said Claude heatedly. "Don't try to lie or haggle with me. Or I shall go elsewhere with the figures."

"Unlikely." Viscera smiled. "The two figures aren't worth that by themselves. To complete the set, yes. And even if you were to steal the entire set from me at gunpoint, what would you do with them? Where would you sell them? You couldn't get them out of England."

"There is a customer right here in London, Viscera."

"You'd never live to reach him," Viscera said amiably. "I know the man to whom you refer. You would have to present him with the complete set and documentation as well. And to take the entire set, monsieur, you would have to kill me and Camion. England is an island. Granted that you could reach the sheik and get the money, you would never escape the British police. No, Monsieur Fitzroi. I am your best and safest customer. I believe we are at what Ms. Fein's countrymen would call a Mexican standoff."

"It's true I might not be able to sell them, Viscera," Claude admitted. "But this does not preclude my breaking up the figurines for the gems, does it?"

"You wouldn't! You couldn't!" Viscera gasped in shock. "It would be an act of unspeakable barbarity!"

"Try me," Claude said, grinning evilly.

Viscera looked from the armoire and its glittering contents to the black muzzle of the revolver Claude held steadily. He heaved a great sigh. "Very well," he said resignedly. "How shall we do this, then?"

"Delighted that you've decided to be reasonable, Viscera," Claude said. He reached into his jacket pocket and took out a piece of paper which he crumpled into a ball and then tossed to Viscera. "You will telephone Zurich and have your agents there disburse the sum we have agreed upon into that account number. I took the precaution of opening this account in the same bank you use. Once it has been done, my agent will call me at this number to confirm it. Then you may have your bloody toys."

"There is no telephone here," Viscera said. "It is upstairs, in the library." He stood up. "Shall we go?"

With Claude and his pistol bringing up the rear, we trooped upstairs to Viscera's library single file, like a family of ducks. As the rest of the rooms in this house, the library was furnished right out of an antique gallery catalog. The only thing that seemed out of place was the telephone, which was Scandinavian and quite modern, though it was concealed inside an antique-looking wooden and leather inlaid chest on an English Renaissance escritoire.

Viscera dialed a number and, after waiting a bit, spoke into the phone in rapid-fire German. I don't speak a word of German, but I recognized from what Yiddish I know that numbers figured heavily in his conversation with Zurich. Numbers in Yiddish are almost the same as in Low German. Viscera ended his conversation and hung up the phone.

"It's done," he said, then sat down behind the escritoire, the chair groaning its protest. He was careful to keep both his hands in sight, on the desk's surface.

"Sehr gut," Claude said, and noting Viscera's raised eyebrows, added, "But of course I speak German. Do you think I would have taken a chance on you trying a ruse?"

Claude had come around from beside Viscera, where he'd stood while Viscera had talked on the phone. For the first time since entering the house, he sat down. Alongside but not within reach of the chair I occupied. Claude Fitzroi, or whatever his name was, was clearly a professional at his seamy trade.

"Now, I suggest we all make ourselves comfortable," he said. "We must wait for the call confirming that the exchange has been made."

"How did you get my personal number?" Viscera asked. Claude only laughed.

"By being one step ahead of you," he replied. "In the same way I got the quartz boyar and the jade cossack out from under your swinish snout." He transferred his gun to his left hand and delicately scratched his nose with his right. "Do you think me some sort of international bungler? I also know the number of your agent in Zurich. Had you dialed any other number, you would be dead by now."

"And you would have been a fugitive from New Scotland Yard," Viscera concluded.

"I wouldn't mention police, were I you," Claude said. "They probably have a full dossier on you. Your drug smuggling from Marseilles, your white slavery in Tangier. They have done their investigation as carefully as I. Of that I am sure."

"Then let us not indulge in name calling," Viscera said with a smile. "But there are a few details that must be taken care of. Ms. Fein here is the first."

"I have thought of that, as well," Claude said, nodding. "She is the one person who can connect all of us. She has seen how the whole operation worked."

"Not much of a problem," said Viscera, who was regaining much of his poise. "We can give her to Camion. He'd like that. Wouldn't you, Pierre?"

Involuntarily, I looked over at Camion. A hard lump formed in the pit of my stomach. The little man was nodding and smiling! I looked to Claude. His face was as unyielding as any of the carved figures in the armoire downstairs.

"That won't be necessary," he said. "And I wouldn't trust that creature of yours with a weapon. No, I have to kill her myself!"

10

"Marvelous!" exclaimed Viscera, his face breaking into a smile. "We seal our bargain in blood, then. Once you have eliminated Ms. Fein, I have the necessary insurance that you will not betray me to the authorities for some hope of a reward. Knowing that you have done a murder, I will have an edge, as Ms. Fein's compatriots say." He sat back in his chair. "All details are covered then. Except for one: the method of Ms. Fein's demise. May I offer a suggestion?"

"By all means," Claude replied.

"Beneath this house," Viscera said, "there is a passageway, quite old, to the London Underground railway system. We are situated at a point close to where the District and Circle Lines meet and curve southward. Do you begin to grasp the potential of the situation, monsieur?"

"I think so. Continue."

"Very well. I suggest that Ms. Fein be taken to the Underground tunnel, close to the nearest platform. The trains are shut down for the night. They will commence running in"—he checked a gold watch on his wrist—"fifty-five minutes. Ms. Fein will be dealt a sharp blow to the head and placed on the tracks, close to a platform. With the morning crowds, the

162

body will not be discovered until after the train leaves the station. And by then, we shall already be on that train, and our separate ways."

"It sounds workable," Claude agreed, as though he were discussing the weather. I couldn't stand it anymore. I got to my feet and screamed at them. "You unspeakable beasts! I'm not meat, to be disposed of! I'm a person, a human being. Have you all sunk so low? No, don't you try to hush me up!" I said to Viscera, seeing him about to speak. "I won't be hushed up! What will you do if I don't? Kill me?"

"There are some things worse than a quick, painless death, Mademoiselle," said Camion with an evil leer. "Why fight the inevitable? If you cause trouble, I shall cause you pain. Pain that you never dreamed could exist."

I swallowed hard at this bit of news and lowered my voice a notch. But I pressed on. "You could do that," I said hotly. "And you'd probably enjoy doing it, too. You're a degenerate. And so are you, Viscera. You're an obscene, slimy, fat slug! You belong under a flat rock!" Then I turned to Claude and looked him straight in the eye. "You're the one I don't understand," I said. "These men are diseased people. They're both physical and emotional freaks. But you, Claude, or whatever your name really is, you're different. You're young. You have an intelligence that could make you a success at anything you tried. You have looks, style, grace!"

"*Ah, merci,* Doris," he said. "You are too kind."

"That's not a compliment, you lowlife!" I snapped. "It's a pity that I could say it. What a dreadful waste of a human being you are! These creatures have no choice about what they do," I said, indicating Viscera and Camion, "but you do. I think it makes you dirtier than they are! And to think that I almost—"

I was about to say that I had almost learned to care for him in Paris. Happily, before I could say it, the telephone on Viscera's desk rang. He spoke into it, again in German. Then he handed the phone to Claude.

"For you, Herr *Gruber,*" he said elaborately, cupping the mouthpiece with one huge hand. "An interesting choice of an alias, I might add."

Claude, or Gruber, took the phone in his free hand and, holding the phone against his chest said, "Don't congratulate yourself, Viscera. I have as many names as you do rolls of fat." Then he broke off, speaking in German. After a few moments, he hung up. "It's been transferred," he said. "Now to the business of Ms. Fein. The sooner it's done, the better. You need but show me the Underground tunnel entrance. I shall do the rest."

"We wouldn't dream of letting you go alone, dear boy," said Viscera. "This house has served its purpose. We shall all go together. Soon, you will be on your way to wherever you wish to go. I shall be on my private jet to a spot in Africa."

I realized then how Camion and Viscera had reached London before Claude/Gruber and I had

arrived. When Camion saw me leave in the cab outside the Colosseum, he must have reported directly
to Viscera. Then knowing where I was supposed to
go, they had taken off for London in Viscera's private
plane.

"But I must dress," Viscera continued. "I am
hardly turned out for traveling. We have only forty-
five minutes left before Ms. Fein's last train arrives.
That done, we shall part, and I hope never to clap
eyes upon you again, Monsieur Fitzroi."

Claude nodded silent agreement. I followed the
huge man and Camion to Viscera's bedroom, where
he dressed. I'd describe the decor of the bedroom to
you in detail, but I can't bring myself to set down the
specifics.

Suffice to say that the walls were covered in black
and gold flocked paper. The vulgar paper was mostly
hidden by framed drawings, etchings, and oil paintings depicting the most revolting scenes of perver-
sity and debauchery imaginable. The bed was huge,
a necessity for a *thing* of Viscera's size. It was cano-
pied and at first I thought it contrasted oddly with
the scabrous wall hangings. The motif was gilded
cherubs, and the footboard in the shape of a swan!
Then I took a closer look. The cherubs were depicted
as aggressively, grotesquely male and were busily
engaged in acts of degradation with each other and
various carved animals. I held my breath, trying not
to vomit as Viscera dressed in street clothing.

Finally, we all went downstairs to the sitting room,

where Viscera transferred the contents of the armoire to two green velvet-lined bags of fine morocco leather. The grips had obviously been designed for the specific purpose of transporting the Romanov collection of figures. Viscera lingered over each piece a second before he put it into its prepared niche inside a bag. He sighed in appreciation as he closed and locked the snaps on the morocco grips. Then he stood erect and said, "Shall we be going?"

With Viscera leading the way, we descended the cellar stairs to the basement of the house. It was a wine cellar. He went directly to one rack of dusty bottles and removed a single flask of wine. With a dry groan, the entire wine rack swung aside to reveal a black tunnel entrance. I could see that it had stairs leading still further downward.

Viscera snapped on a small flashlight, of the sort one sees on key chains in luggage stores. He began descending the stairs. We followed, and the second that Claude, as the last person in the group stepped inside, the door behind us swung shut.

"Ingenious, isn't it?" said Viscera descending, his voice echoing spookily. "The previous owner of the house dug below his wine cellar as a precaution when the Nazis were bombing London in World War II. Once I discovered it, I merely extended his excavation to where I had access to the Underground railway tunnel."

"Convenient," said Claude from behind me. "It

allows anyone to come and go from your house and not be seen."

"And transport certain contraband items as well," Viscera called back cheerily. "One may disappear neatly into the crowd at the Underground station. Or contrariwise, disappear from the Underground and gain access to my house."

I guess it was Viscera's use of "contrariwise," which is an *Alice in Wonderland* word, that made me think of something out of my early childhood. My parents had taken me to Disneyland. I was only six years old. There had been one of those actors that Disneyland hires dressed up as the White Rabbit from *Alice*. I suppose to an adult those getups, with their grotesque papier-mâché heads and costumed bodies, look cutsie-poo. But when you're only four feet tall and an impressionable, imaginative six-year-old, they are scary! And now, I felt like Alice going deeper and deeper into the rabbit hole, with Viscera a pink rabbit.

Viscera paused in front of us, and I was unprepared for the stop. I bumped into Camion's back and recoiled in disgust from coming in contact with him. Viscera worked some sort of latch and a door swung open directly onto a subway train tunnel! We stepped into the darkness, guided only by Viscera's flashlight ahead of us. Picking our way carefully along the walkway, we followed the bobbing circle of light cast by Viscera's pocket torch. After a few minutes' walk, my eyes became accustomed to the darkness, and I could make out the reflections of light thrown as Viscera's flash glinted off the rails on the tunnel floor.

"There's the third rail," Viscera called back. "There's no power in it just now, but soon the electricity will be switched on."

As if on cue, the tunnel grew bright. Small-wattage light bulbs came on, set into the walls of the walkway where we were and that workmen use. Also, the red, amber, and green signal lights for the trains came on. Viscera switched off his flashlight.

"We must hurry," he said. "A train will be due any minute."

We accelerated our pace. And just as we approached a bend in the tunnel, Viscera stopped abruptly. The effect was like a rear-end pileup on a freeway at rush hour. We knocked together in series of fleshy thumps. At the same time, Viscera ducked low and shouted, "Now, Camion!"

The evil little man seemed to melt away from in front of me. Simultaneously, I heard the *click* as his switchblade snapped open. Claude had searched him too hurriedly and been satisfied finding the gun. He'd missed getting Camion's terrible knife! I was directly between Claude and Camion, an unenviable place to be.

With a wordless cry, I pushed myself off the walkway of the tunnel and away from my captors. The third rail with its high voltage didn't frighten me.

That was only a *possible* death. No matter who won this scuffle in the tunnel, I was dead unless I could get away while they were busy!

I miscalculated where the wall was, though. I felt a sharp pain in my elbow, then saw Claude's gun clatter to the floor of the tunnel, inches from the third rail. I'd accidently knocked it from his hand! I lost my balance and sat down heavily on the roadbed, between the two nonelectrical rails.

Viscera saw it too. He turned and shone his flashlight, much brighter than the bulbs set in the walls, directly into Claude's face, as Camion closed in with his knife. Momentarily blinded, Claude threw an arm in front of his face, and I saw Camion's blade enter Claude's body, stomach high, on the right side!

Claude gave a low groan, but brought his raised right arm straight across in a vicious blade-handed karate blow that ended neatly and meatily below Pierre Camion's nose, still moving upward. I've gone to enough Kung-Fu movies with Larry Small to recognize the shot. It was not a blow to disable. It was deathblow! The small bones of the nose are driven up into the brain and cause almost instant death.

Camion cried out and, from the force of Claude's blow, reeled backward, into Viscera. The little man's hand still clutched the handle of the long switchblade knife. He fell heavily against Viscera, then tumbled toward the tracks, feet from where I sat, still watching in horror. As Camion fell, some last fleeting glimmer of life must have caused him to grab at anything nearby to break his fall. What he grabbed was Gaspar Viscera's leg.

Have you ever had some joker in gym class do that trick where they knock against the back of your knee and your whole leg buckles? That's the spot where Camion struck Viscera as he fell to the tracks. Off balance and burdened by the two grips containing the figurines, Viscera wobbled crazily as Camion fell. But my eyes were on Camion.

The little man fell spread-eagled across the tracks; his outflung hand with the knife still clutched in it rapped against one rail, and then the tip of the knife blade came into contact with the high-voltage-charged third rail!

A fat blue spark arced from rail to knife and, abruptly, Camion's body was bathed in a pale blue St. Elmo's fire. I let out a yelp, but I was in no danger. I was far enough away and out of reach of the killer current that played about Camion's body, crackling and coruscating in the dim light of the tunnel.

I heard an animal cry and looked up. Gaspar Viscera was still teetering on the edge of the walkway, desperately trying to regain his balance. Self-preservation finally overcame his greed, and he let loose the two grips containing the Fabergé figures. But it was too late. He fell heavily, and I shall never forget the look on his face as he descended helplessly toward the mass of burning flesh and arcing electricity that once had been Pierre Camion.

Viscera gave one last scream, then he came in contact with the seared mess on the tunnel floor. The electric sparks bloomed, then raged about this new bit of fuel. The smell of burning hair and flesh filled the tunnel, making my stomach turn over.

Then suddenly, some sort of automatic circuit breaker must have cut out. Abruptly, the tunnel was plunged into darkness and the hell fire of high-voltage current stopped crackling about the forms of the little man and Viscera, now joined in death. For a few seconds, all I could see in the dark was the retinal memory of that awful electric flame. Then I saw the still-burning electric torch Viscera had dropped before he fell! I scrambled to my feet and grabbed it. As fast as I could, I got back on the tracks and, in the beam of the flash, located the fallen pistol. Knowing that the current was off in the third rail, I scooped up the pistol and whirled to locate Claude Fitzroi. He was still standing, leaning against the tunnel wall, his hand clutched to his side, where Camion's knife had pierced him. I aimed the gun at Fitzroi the way I'd seen him do it: two hands and dead-on steady.

"Make a move I don't tell you to, and you're dead!" I shouted.

"I couldn't move if I wanted to," groaned Fitzroi. "Give me a hand, will you?"

"I wouldn't touch you with a fork!" I snapped. I aimed the gun straight at his head.

He groaned again, and held out one hand. "Help me, Doris," he moaned.

"Don't try to sucker me, you phony Frenchman!"

I said. "I saw where Camion stabbed you. You're not that hurt. You just pick up those two bags with the figures in them. We're going back to that town house!"

I maneuvered the small flashlight between the fingers of my left hand, so that wherever I pointed the light, the gun was automatically aimed. I prayed I wouldn't have to use it. I've never held a gun in my hand in my entire life. I wondered idly about that safety catch thing they always talk about in movies. But I think that's just on automatics, not revolvers. I pulled back the hammer with my thumb.

"All right, all right," Fitzroi said. He walked over and picked up the two bags. I'd been right! He wasn't all that badly off. He was trying to get me close enough so he could grab the gun.

"Now, march!" I said, and off we went.

"You don't understand the true situation, Doris," he said to me as we reentered the wine cellar. "I'm not what you think."

"It's lucky for you that you don't know what I think," I replied. "But you'll find out, once I call the London police!"

"Oh no!" cried Fitzroi. "You'll screw it all up if you call the cops!"

As he spoke these words, I realized with a shock that he'd completely lost his French accent! He sounded like an American! In fact, I was beginning to recognize that voice. It was the accent that had misled me. It was the voice that had given me my telephone instructions in Rome!

"He's quite right, you know," said a bass-baritone voice from the head of the wine cellar stairs. "You'll ruin everything if you blow the whistle." I looked up and, sitting on the top step in his elf-on-a-mushroom pose, was Cody Garrett! Standing behind him was a very large, very clean-cut chap. Garrett arched his brows at me.

"Were you to shoot him, Ms. Fein," he added, "I'd lose one of my best agents. And as you know, good help is so terribly hard to get."

11

"You lied!" I shouted into the telephone the next day. "You've never been honest with me for a second!"

"There's nothing in the rules that says you had to know the whole truth," came back George Case's voice over the transatlantic telephone connection. "The Organization operates on a need-to-know basis."

"Well, there are certain things a courier should know," I answered. "Like: Is my life in danger? That's just for openers!"

"If your life was in jeopardy, it was part of the job," said Case coldly. "Danger comes with the territory."

"I didn't even know there was a territory," I said. "I didn't know anything. You just threw me to the lions. Or I should say the jackals!"

"You were never really alone," Case said. "Fitzroi was following you in a cab, masquerading as a driver. If you had known that when Camion snatched you in Rome, you would have spilled everything you knew. Your very ignorance of the plan was additional life insurance. The closest you came to real danger was running through Roman traffic. Fitzroi had been watching the entrance you took into the Colosseum, thinking you'd come out the same way. When you didn't he began circling the block, checking exits. Luckily, he spotted you before some crazy Roman driver ran you down."

I fell silent for a moment. Case was right. In the grip of that terrible little man, I would have told all. And if I hadn't, I probably would have invented something. And once I had, my usefulness to Viscera would have been over. So would my life have been. But I didn't want to concede so much as a hair. I was hopping mad about the way I had been treated. I'd said as much to Cody Garrett that frightening morning when I nearly shot Claude Fitzroi. Actually, I shouldn't keep calling him that. I found out his real name from Garrett a few minutes after I led Claude at gunpoint into the cellar of the town house in Belgravia.

"His name is Francis X. McMahon," Garrett had said in his grumbly-low voice. "New York born and Paris educated. The accent comes naturally to him, Ms. Fein. His mother was a Parisian."

"I have certain other ideas about his ancestry," I countered, "but I'm too polite to voice them in public."

"Have a heart, Doris," Claude/Gruber/McMahon wheedled. "You weren't in danger of death. I held the gun at all times. Until you knocked it out of my hand, that is," he added pointedly.

"That was purely accidental," I defended. "And how could I have known you were working on the side of the IGO? I could have shot you, you know."

"Oh, I think not," Garrett said easily. "Our psychological profile on you indicates a strong commitment to nonviolence."

"My what?" I cried. "You mean to tell me that you have a file on my personality? How dare you!"

"How dare we not?" said Garrett. "We have a file on anyone who so much as licks postage stamps for the Organization. You came highly recommended, if that's a consolation to you. George Case himself said he thought you could blossom into a fine agent. Once you got rid of some unnecessary, outdated morality, that is."

"Gee, thanks," I said elaborately. "You mean like truth, loyalty, and integrity? I'd rather keep what I've got."

"Is it still necessary that you keep the pistol?" asked Claude. "My side feels like I've been stuck with a red hot poker and I . . ." Slowly, and with that same charming smile I had believed in Paris, Claude sank to the floor of the cellar. It was only then that I saw the extent of the red stain that began at his waist and had soaked the upper part of his trousers. The dark color of his slacks had concealed the fact that the man had been bleeding steadily. Suddenly I felt awful. I dropped the revolver to the floor of the wine cellar and rushed to him.

"Claude!" I cried. "I'm sorry, I didn't realize!"

He moaned and opened his eyes for a moment, saying, "I'm sorry, kid. We do what we have to. . . . But for what it's worth, I wasn't acting all that hard in Paris. . . . I really do care . . . I . . ." Then he passed out. I looked up at Garrett and the large clean-cut type at the head of the stairs.

"Well, don't just stand there!" I said. "Get a doctor! Do something besides sit there and smirk like a smug leprechaun!"

Garrett laughed aloud. "All right, Ms. Fein," he said. Then to the huge muscular type, "Cooper, help McMahon. Take him to the Organization doctor. The usual rates and forms."

The big man descended the cellar stairs in eerie silence. I noted that for all his size, he came down the stairs with the grace of a dancer. He bent over the fallen Claude—I *must* stop calling him that: McMahon—and picked him up as though he were a child. The last I saw of McMahon, he was carried off in the arms of the strong man named Cooper.

"I'm sure that you have many questions, Ms. Fein," Garrett said. "I have equally as many. There is certain data I need immediately, and McMahon is in no shape to tell me."

"Debriefing?" I said, remembering the three days I'd spent in a cabin on a lake outside New York after the Dakama affair.

"Exactly," said Garrett, smiling. "You're picking up the jargon, aren't you?"

"I'm picking up my right foot," I said. "And after I put it down, I'm picking up the left. In case you're not familiar with the process, it's called walking. I'm walking straight out of here and to my hotel. Or to a cab that will take me there. As to your debriefing, you'll get what I know when I'm good and ready to tell you. And I don't say a word until I've had a bath and a change of clothes." I began ascending the stairs, where Garrett still sat like an evil elf. I was telling the truth, too. I was sick to death of the IGO and all it stood for. If I'd had any sense, I would have collapsed like Cl—like *McMahon* had.

The little man stood up and blocked my way. "I can't let you go until I know where Viscera and Camion are. I assume that the two bags you have there contain the Fabergé collection?"

"Camion and Viscera are dead," I said, still climbing the stairs. "Electrocuted on the third rail of the subway. You can reach the Underground through this tunnel. That's how Viscera worked his smuggling route." By this time, I was one step below where Garrett stood. With the differential in our heights, we were almost at eye level. I took off the raincoat that Garrett had loaned me in Paris. By now, it was not only filthy, but torn in several places. The way I figured it, the IGO owed Gretchen Hinman, its owner, a brand-new raincoat.

"Here's the coat I borrowed," I said to the diminutive diplomat. Without warning, I moved like a bullfighter and threw the coat capelike over the head of Cody Garrett. While he was momentarily taken aback, I climbed to the stair above him, spun him about, and planted a swift kick in the seat of his impeccably tailored trousers. He tumbled down the stairs with a series of satisfying thumps. He came to rest at the foot of the stairs and, after a comic few seconds, disentangled the borrowed raincoat from his head and shoulders. I noted the addled look on his face with satisfaction.

"That's for the lies and treachery!" I said from the doorway. "If you want any more information, I'll be at the Hyde Park Hotel!"

It was childish, I suppose, but what of it? I'd been jerked around by these people, the supposed "good guys," for the better part of a week. And in every contact I'd had with the IGO, whether in New York on the Dakama affair or on this crazy odyssey. I was filled with rage and frustration. Garrett was as good as anyone to take it out on. I only wished in my heart that it could have been one George Case!

"Are you still there, Doris?" came Case's voice over the thousands of miles. "Hello? Hello?"

"I'm still here," I said. "What more do you want to know?" I'd been on the phone for over an hour now. Garrett had known better than to contact me in person. After I'd had a day and a night's sleep, a breakfast tray and a dozen red roses had arrived at my room at the Hyde Park Hotel. The card had read: *Mea culpa,* and was signed simply, *Garrett.*

I'd just finished some excellent kippers and coffee when the phone had rung. It was Case. He wanted the information I hadn't given to Garrett. Told me that one of his agents was on the hotel switchboard and that it was safe to speak. I made him sweat until he gave me some answers.

"Who tore up all my new wardrobe?" I demanded.

"Garrett," said Case. "In fact, he was late getting to your suite at the Henri IV. He's a real diplomat, you know. He was delayed at a function. You came in on time and nearly caught him in the act. At that point, he still had the quartz boyar in his coat pocket."

"That lying so-and-so," I said. "Do you know what a fool he made of me?"

"No one can make a fool of you without your helping in some way," countered Case laconically. "Now, will you answer my questions?"

"No!" I shouted into the phone. "I no longer work for your lying, rotten Organization! I'll tell you when I feel like it! First, I want some more answers!"

"This is blackmail," said Case. I could hear anger beginning in his voice.

"Precisely," I said smugly. "And you should recognize blackmail when you hear it. You use it often enough: real or emotional blackmail. The idea! You told me about plant enzymes!"

"That's an old agency gag," Case began.

"I know what it is. Garrett told me," I snapped.

"You know, he sprained his ankle when you knocked him down those stairs," Case said.

"Don't try to blackmail me emotionally, Case," I said. "I saw how he landed. He bumped down the stairs on the same spot I kicked him. If he's hurt, it's only in the . . . pride."

Case laughed. "You're getting too sharp to be manipulated easily, aren't you, Doris?"

"You bet I am," I replied. "And you won't flatter me into what you want, either!"

"Touché," said Case. "I feel glad now that I took your Uncle Claude's advice."

"Who?" I squeaked.

"Your Uncle Claude Bernard," Case replied. "He knows the profession well. He should. He's the head of the Dakaman intelligence section. He trained right here in Maryland, at our Academy. He has one of the best intelligence networks in all Africa."

"That's why those terrorists were after him and my Aunt Lois!" I said in sudden realization. "I couldn't understand back then why they wanted to kidnap an economic attaché . . ." A bright light dawned over me. If it had been a cartoon, I would have had a light bulb drawn over my head! "Wait a minute," I said. "That's Garrett's title, too!"

"You got it, sister," said Case. "Economic attaché is the standard cover for any bureau chief. It's one of those open secrets in the business."

"Like the plant-growth enzyme?" I asked sarcastically.

"Exactly," said Case, ignoring my tone.

"And tell me," I said, "why the lies about the Fabergé collection? The agency never did have all but two of the figures. Two figures were all you had!"

"True," Case admitted. "We suspected that Viscera had the rest of them. But he's like, or was like, a
pack rat with holes in many different corners of the
world. They could have been anywhere from Macao
to London. All we would have done if we'd tried a
break-in would have been to make him hide them
better and deeper. We counted on his love of the
workmanship. Knew that if we could get the other
two into his possession, without his suspecting it was
a plant, he'd have to put them together. Just to look
at the collection intact."

"And used me as a cat's-paw to do it, you lowlife!"
I said.

"The importance of the mission justified it," Case
said flatly. "One of the hazards of the spy game,
Doris."

"You took some unnecessary risks with my life," I
said hotly. "Clau—McMahon had Viscera, Camion,
and the collection at gunpoint. It was all over right
there. There was no need to go through that horrid
scene in the Underground tunnel."

"Oh, but there was," Case answered. "We'd been
watching all Viscera's ratholes. But we never could
figure out how he was getting contraband in and out
of the Belgravia house. And as Camion and Viscera
are dead now, and the rest of Viscera's organization
doesn't know . . ."

"You can catch them as they come popping in

from the tunnel," I concluded.

"Absolutely," said Case. "Your uncle was right. And I agree. You have the makings of a first-class agent, Doris."

"If you think that's a compliment, think again," I answered. "I wouldn't touch your rotten outfit with a fork!"

"McMahon was protecting you," protested Case. "And we had two other men at the Colosseum in Rome."

"And let that little monster Camion shoot one of them," I put in. "That was the coldest thing I've ever seen in my life!"

"That was one hundred percent *your* fault," said Case quickly. "We had no idea that you were going to turn heroic on us."

"It wasn't courage," I said. "It was sheer desperation and anger. Just about the way I feel now," I added pointedly.

"Whatever you want to call it," Case said, "you *did* act bravely. By the way, the courier will live. And you also acted efficiently in the Underground tunnel. Tell me truthfully, Doris. Would you really have shot McMahon?"

"I don't know," I admitted. "I think if he had tried to grab the gun, I *might* have."

"Good girl!" said Case warmly. "There's hope for you as a full agent."

"I'm not a girl!" I snapped angrily. "I'm a grown

woman. I make my own decisions. And the first one is that I won't have anything to do with you or the IGO. If I live to be eighty!"

"Don't be hasty just because you've been through a lot," wheedled Case. "We'll make it up to you."

"Never!" I rejoined.

"Too bad," Case said, and I could see his mirthless smile in my mind's eye. "We've replaced your wardrobe down to the last item. Your measurements are on record at our New York shops now. We wired the list to London. In about an hour or two, your luggage will arrive at the Hyde Park. Along with the rest of your traveler's checks. You left most of them in Paris, you know."

I didn't say anything. The truth was, I'd forgotten all about them. I realized in a rush that I hadn't contacted any of the names on Uncle Claude's list in Paris. I hadn't called my parents, either. They must be mad with worry, I thought. I mentioned that to George Case.

"Not to worry," he said. "We sent a cable in your name to your parents in New York. And another from Rome. You're covered."

"And what kind of cable would you have sent if Camion had killed me?" I asked nastily. "A singing message?"

"I won't comment on that," Case said quickly. "And I don't think you want an answer, either. Now, can we get on with the debriefing?"

"Not until I see my luggage and traveler's checks,"

I answered. "You owe me my vacation and, by all that's holy, I'm going to have it!" I hung up and returned my attention to what was left of my breakfast.

My baggage, identical to the cases Garrett had slashed in Paris, arrived two and a half hours later. I checked the contents, and every last item was there. Not surprising. The IGO had a complete list. The phone rang minutes later. It was Case.

"All right, you have your things," he said without preamble. "Now let's start talking about what happened. I have a list of questions."

He certainly did. Half an hour later, I was still talking.

". . . And that's about it," I concluded.

"Fine, just fine, Ms. Fein." The head of the IGO snickered at his unintentional joke. "There will be more questions later, from Garrett. But I have all I needed to know immediately. Enjoy your European vacation."

"I'll enjoy it, all right," I said grimly. "After I have a little chat with that phony Frenchman you sent to romance me in Paris."

"No problem there," Case said easily. "He's due for rest and recuperation after that knife wound. We thought you might appreciate a trained European guide. McMahon speaks five languages, and he has lived all over the continent. . . ."

"I wouldn't go anywhere with that lying skunk!" I snapped. "Unless it was to his funeral!" My ego was still smarting from how easily he had batted his baby blue eyes at me and led me anywhere he wanted.

"Really?" said Case archly. "He spoke so highly of you. Let me see, in his report he says: *'In my estimation, Doris Fein is a young woman of above average intelligence. She consistently displayed initiative and courage in the course of the mission. Were she a regular agent, I would recommend her for a decoration. Further, she is a charming and personable woman of very attractive persuasion. She could, with training, be a high-level agent.'* Now what do say to that, Doris?" Case asked.

"Not much," I replied. "I'm still mad at him. And I don't know if you made all that up. I never know when you're lying."

"Why don't you ask him yourself, then?" Case inquired. "He's in the room adjoining yours at the Hyde Park."

"Where?"

"Right next door to you, Doris. He's recovering very nicely from the wound. It was just the fleshy part of his side. Lot of blood, but no internal puncture to speak of. Oh, he's in some pain, but that doesn't matter to you, does it?"

"Of course not," I lied. "It comes with the territory, doesn't it?"

Case laughed loud and long. I think it was the first genuine laugh I'd heard from him since we'd met. "That's the spirit!" he chortled. "You'll be a top agent yet!"

"Not on your grandma, I won't!" I said to Case. "I'm going to enjoy my vacation. And when that's done, I'm due to start my college education at the University of California, in Irvine. Incidentally, did you know my major is in journalism? I may write all this down. I'm sure someone would publish it."

"You wouldn't! You couldn't!" protested Case. "We'll take steps to prevent it! We'll—"

I hung up while Case was still spluttering. Of course I wasn't going to expose the IGO. I was mad, but my country is my country. Outfits like the IGO shouldn't exist, I suppose. But as long as their counterparts exist in other countries, we'd be fools here in America not to have protection against them.

I looked at the telephone. So Francis X. McMahon was in the room right next to mine! I ought to call and tell him off properly, I thought. He's got it coming, Lord knows. But then a voice from somewhere in my head—or was it my heart?—said, "But he's hurt. He's in pain!"

I thought of the grand night we'd had in Paris. And I also thought of what he'd said, lying there on the floor of the wine cellar: "I really do care . . ." In that moment, I made a decision. Francis McMahon and I had some unfinished business.

I began sorting through the second edition of my new wardrobe, looking for exactly the right thing to wear. After all, a phone call is so impersonal. And he *was* right down the hall. . . .